Room Enough

Copyright © 2023 Roger Truitt

All rights reserved. No part of this publication may be reproduced, distributed, or transmitted in any form or by any means, including photocopying, recording, or other electronic or mechanical methods, without the prior written permission of the publisher, except in the case of brief quotations embodied in critical reviews and certain other noncommercial uses permitted by copyright law. For permission requests, write to the publisher at: roomenoughbook@gmail.com.

ISBN: 979-8-218-21093-9 (Paperback)

Library of Congress Control Number: 2023909107

This book is a work of historical fiction. Any references to historical events, real people, or real places are used fictitiously. Other names, characters, places and events are products of the author's imagination, and any resemblance to actual events, places or persons, living or dead, is entirely coincidental. See Author's Postscript for more details.

Front Cover Images & Cover Design by Laura Navarre.
Book Interior Design by Heimat Publishing, Crystal Heidel.

Printed in the United States of America.

First printing edition 2023.

Room Enough

Wm. Roger Truitt

DEDICATION

Room Enough is dedicated to my grandparents, James Henry and Bessie Shockley Truitt, my parents, James Shockley and Dorothy Shockley Truitt, and my wife, Patricia Truitt.

In 1908 my grandparents bought a 23-acre farm just outside of the town limits of Rehoboth Beach, where my father was born. He spent his early married life with my mother in a refurbished camp meeting house on Baltimore Avenue. That same tiny frame cottage become the Anna Hazzard Tent House Museum located on Christian Street, where the author occasionally appears as an 1870s-costumed Rev. Todd.

Patricia encouraged me to rediscover the history of my hometown, to play the character of Rev. Robert Todd for the Rehoboth Beach Historical Society, and to research, draft, and edit the manuscript. Patricia also is an aspiring author and docent for the Rehoboth Art League's Peter Marsh Homestead, who understands and appreciates the time commitment required to complete a labor of love. She has been a patient and valuable sounding board and contributor to many scenes in the story.

W.R.T.

ACKNOWLEDGMENTS

Thanks to *Dr. Michael Kardos* for his guidance, encouragement, and excellent help in editing the manuscript. Kudos to my daughter *Laura Navarre*, who designed the cover and enhanced the photographs. Heimat Publishing's *Crystal Heidel* provided wonderful support with proofreading and interior book design. Additionally, I am grateful to the following for their time, expertise, and/or valuable feedback on the manuscript.

Nancy Alexander, Director, Rehoboth Beach Historical Society and Museum

Paul Lovett, Rehoboth Beach Historian, Author and Lecturer

Sterling Street, Coordinator, Nanticoke Indian Association

Rev. Dr. Jonathan Baker, Retired Pastor of Rehoboth Beach Epworth United Methodist Church

Denise Clemons, Archivist, Lewes Historical Society

Barbara Duffin and *Philip Lawton*, Barratt's Chapel Museum

Russell McCabe, Delaware State Archivist (retired)

Rev. Earle Baker, Retired Pastor of Lewes Bethel United Methodist Church

John Gauger, Rehoboth Beach Epworth United Methodist Church Historian

Carl Pierce, Board Member, Rehoboth Beach Historical Society

Finally, *Donna Baker* and *Peggi Zelinko* provided valuable assistance reading and editing the final draft of the manuscript.

AUTHOR'S NOTE

Readers should be aware that the scenes, language and action in *Room Enough* are symbolic of what likely would have been experienced by persons living in the mid-late nineteenth century in Sussex County Delaware. That is not to suggest that such activities and terminology were appropriate then or now.

W.R.T.

FOREWORD

In *Room Enough*, Roger Truitt has accurately and sensitively addressed the significant history of the development of the Methodist Camp Meeting in Rehoboth Beach, with the cultural diversity and challenges this movement experienced from its inception. Having grown up in the Delaware eastern shore as the son and grandson of Methodist pastors and having served as a United Methodist pastor for 41 years, the book transported me to people and places I had heard about and experienced during my life. As pastor of the Epworth United Methodist Church in Rehoboth Beach for 20 years, I experienced anew in this book the beauty and the challenges the shore area brings when people come together from various cultural and religious backgrounds and confront racism and other prejudices that have existed for generations. Any reader will discover what happens when people, open to God's Spirit, accept each other and develop meaningful relationships. Roger Truitt reminds us that "Rehoboth" (Genesis 26:22) is a place where there is room for all.

Rev. Dr. Jonathan Baker

LEWES AND REHOBOTH

Sussex Co.

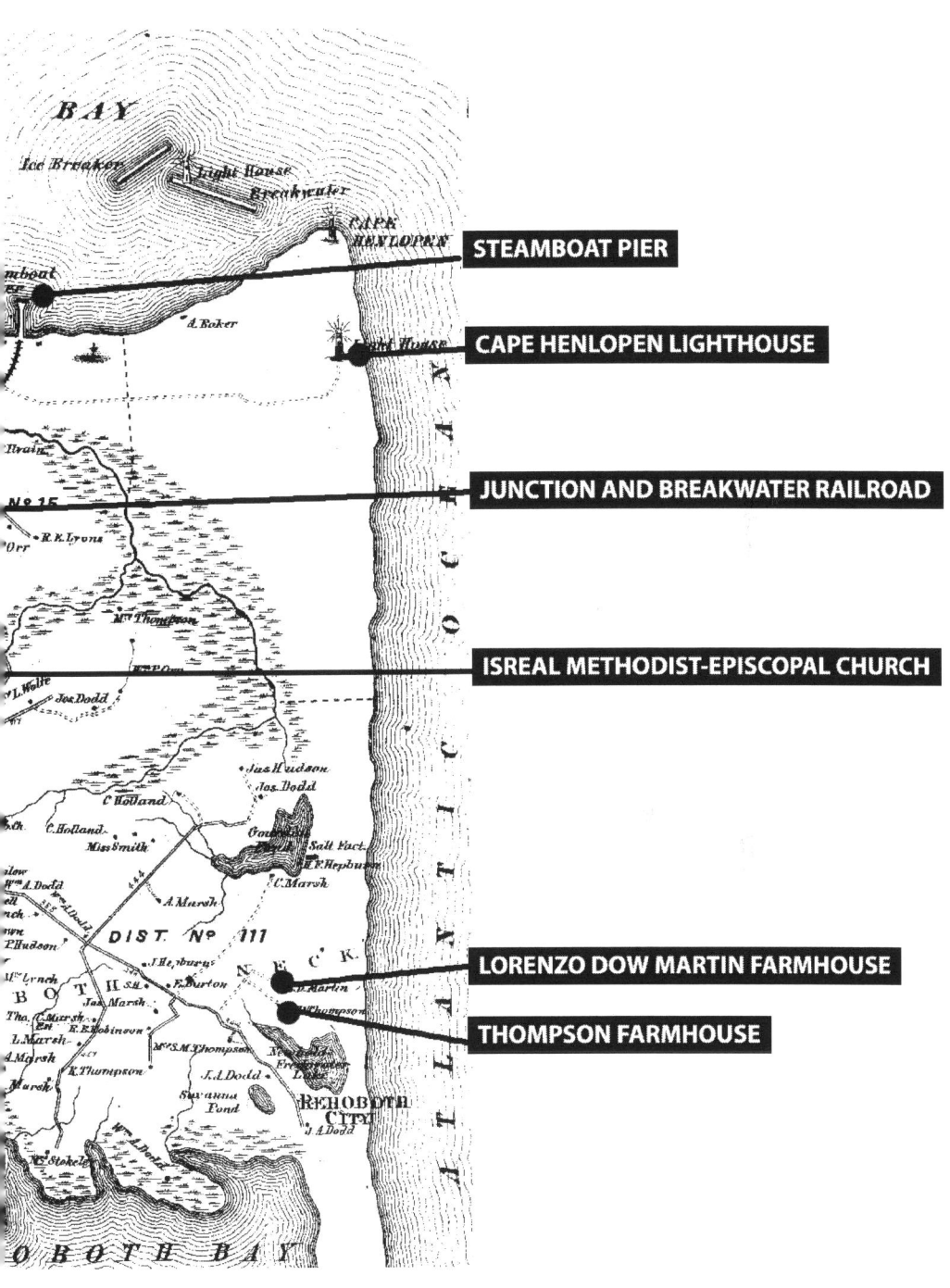

Lewes and Rehoboth Hundred (base map is *circa* 1868, Pomeroy and Beers Atlas, from Delaware Geological Survey website).

Chapter One

ROAD TO ZOAR

August, 1871
Rehoboth Neck, Delaware

WILL THOMPSON HOISTED the fifth basket of ruby red tomatoes onto the horse-drawn wagon with a grunt. He pulled a red bandana from the back pocket of his overalls and wiped his sweating forehead as the noonday sun beat down on him like a blast furnace.

Elizabeth pushed open the screen door of their modest farmhouse with a shout, carrying a steaming cast-iron kettle with a towel wrapped around its hot handle. "Will, don't forget to take these boiled chickens with you to the camp meeting grounds. Everyone will be starving after such a long day."

As she handed the kettle to Will to load onto the wagon, she surveyed the tomatoes and added, "Where are the fresh cucumbers and sweet corn I asked you to pick?"

Will glared at his wife. She did this every year during the camp meetings at Zoar, insisting he drop everything and deliver food to the ministers and parishioners at the revival services.

"You treat these religious crazies better than your own husband. We could make some real good money on all the food you give away." They needed the money to support the three girls and Willie. She knew that. "Every year at this time it's the same thing. I'm gettin' sick and tired of it."

"Now, Will," Elizabeth said calmly. "You know how important it is to me and our children to show Christian love in giving to others without any expectation of receiving anything back. Since you never go to church or read the Good Book, you just can't understand why we're called to do this."

Now his six-mile trip to the market in Lewes would have to wait until tomorrow, all because she'd begged him to take food to the religious nuts at Zoar.

Will raised his voice another octave and looked sternly at his wife. "I sure do understand I've been sweatin' like a hog in heat pickin' our best ripe vegetables to give away to people I don't know or care about."

He had gotten up at dawn to milk their two cows, feed the pigs and chickens, and clean the manure out of the chicken house. Then he picked ten bushels of corn, three crates of tomatoes, and two bushels of green beans to take from his Rehoboth Neck farm to the market in Lewes. "And now you 'spect me to take the wagon eight miles to feed some God damned lazy fools preachin' and singin' instead of workin' like me?"

"Will, please calm down. The children are listening," Elizabeth whispered as she embraced his sweat-drenched shoulder with one arm. "And take Willie with you. It will be good for the two of you to spend some time together. The girls and I need to prepare for Sunday school this week."

Will wiped his brow again with the soaked handkerchief. He squinted at the boiling sun and breathed in and out deeply. There was no winning this. "Tell Willie to stop playin' the piano, and get Buddy hitched up while I get the cukes and corn."

Will returned with several baskets of ripe cucumbers and sweet corn and placed them carefully on the back of the wagon as Willie slid the harness over Buddy's head and fastened the straps under his hefty belly and hindquarters. Willie spoke gently to Buddy as he placed the bit into the horse's mouth by depressing his lower jaw with his thumb. Will grabbed his rifle and slid it under the seat.

Elizabeth reappeared to see them off. "Be sure to look up Reverend Todd and let him know the children and I plan to attend tomorrow's services. You better get a move on to make it to the campground before supper time."

"You know Buddy's no spring chicken!" Will shouted back to Elizabeth as the old buckboard wagon rolled away in a cloud of dust.

Willie settled into the seat next to his father, resting his tattered leather shoes on the buckboard. They turned onto the dirt road toward Lewes. "Pop, how old is Buddy?"

Will had to think about it. "'bout twenty," he said. "I inherited him when my pop had a heart attack and died. I 'member Buddy as a powerful and unbroken stallion before we gelded him."

"Gelded?"

Will knew right away he shouldn't have mentioned that word. Though probably it was time to talk to Willie about such things. The boy was almost thirteen.

He paused as the wagon rumbled down the dirt road in the ruts made by hundreds of wooden wagon wheels before them. The breeze created by the movement of the wagon felt good to Will, and his sweat-drenched shirt finally was drying out.

"What does gelded mean Pop?"

"Means we cut him to calm him down," Will said.

"Cut him?"

"Me and your uncle George tied him up and held him down," Will said matter-of-factly, "while my father used a knife to cut off his balls."

"That must have hurt Buddy real bad," Willie said, clenching his knees together. "I'd hate to see him in pain."

"It hurt him for a few days, but he healed up. Then we could use him as a work horse on the farm."

Willie was quiet for the next few minutes as they passed the Presbyterian Church at Midway and turned west onto the Millsboro Road. "Did Buddy want to jump on mares like I see the stallions do over at Uncle George's farm?"

Will wondered why Willie asked so many questions, but figured they couldn't talk about these things around the girls. "Not after we gelded him. He lost interest in all that."

"Uncle George says his stallions are going to breed the best racehorses in the county. Did Buddy breed any racehorses?"

"Hell, no! No time or money for horse racin'. And don't you ever mention your uncle's race horses to me again."

After nearly an hour at a fast trot along the smooth dirt road, Buddy's nostrils flared and sweat dripped down his neck. Willie noticed Buddy's anguish and begged his father to go easy. As they turned off the main road, the ride became bumpy and Will pulled on the reins to slow Buddy down.

"Pop, how long will Buddy live?"

"Hard to know. He's slowin' down and not eatin' much. His teeth don't look good."

Will knew Buddy wasn't going to be able to pull the wagon to market many more seasons. Without a reliable horse, he wondered how he would provide for his family. Will hoped Buddy would hang on at least until the three girls got married and were someone else's responsibility. It just wasn't fair that he had four mouths to feed and George had just one son who was old enough to take care of himself.

"What will happen to Buddy when he dies?" Willie asked.

"Well, son, we'll bury him to keep the buzzards off. Don't need to worry about that till it happens."

Willie flinched, and his chin began to quiver. "I mean, will I see him in Heaven?"

Will turned and made eye contact with his son. "I know your mother believes in all that Heaven crap, but I think it's a bunch of foolish talk."

"So what do you think happens to us after we die?"

Will had seen a lot of good men shot in the Civil War and left to die and rot in a field or buried in mass graves. He could still smell the rotting flesh.

He thought back to his father's funeral four years earlier, when the hired preacher joked about dead folks becoming worm food and his older brother George had laughed right along with the preacher. George had always scoffed at religious folks.

Will's father had never gone to church or believed in Heaven, or at least they never talked about it. His mother had died in childbirth when Will was four years old. Far as he knew, she never went to church either or believed in an afterlife. The only time he'd been inside a church was when Elizabeth insisted that he attend the children's baptisms. She took the children to Bethel Church in Lewes every Sunday. He refused to go.

"Nothin', son," he said. "Nothin' happens. We rot in the ground, and that's it."

"But what about our souls? Mama believes our soul goes either to Heaven or Hell depending on how good a Christian we've been."

"That's a bunch of poppycock to make us not worry so much about dyin'. The only thing that matters afterwards is what people say about us. So you best be good and not kill anybody or steal from others. You understand?"

But his answer was another question. "Why'd you bring your rifle with us? Are we going huntin'?"

Willie had never shown any interest in guns or hunting. "No, but I like to have it handy in case there's any trouble. Would you like to learn how to shoot it?"

They continued along at a slow pace. Buddy seemed to appreciate the easier gait on the bumpy road. "I don't think I'd like shooting animals," Willie said. "Mama says they're God's creatures."

"Look, if there were a God, don't you think he put them animals here for us to kill and eat? Your Mama ain't 'fraid for me to kill a chicken for dinner is she?"

"No, but that's different. The chickens aren't out in the wild. I think God provided the chickens for our food."

Will wondered why his own namesake – William James Thompson, Jr. – was not like him or his father before him or his brother's son. Willie would rather play the piano Elizabeth inherited from her parents than do outside chores or hunt like the other boys his age. He seemed to be too sensitive and would get upset and cry at the drop of a hat.

The afternoon sun was getting lower in the sky and making it harder to see the road ahead as they traveled west towards the campground. Will knew they needed to get there soon or he would never hear the end of it. He loosened the reins and urged Buddy to pick it up for the last two miles.

As they rounded a bend, they encountered a flock of buzzards feasting on a dead possum in the middle of the road. Buddy dug his hoofs into the soft soil, spooked by the buzzards taking flight and the possum directly in his path. The old horse stumbled and fell sideways. Buddy's abrupt stop threw Willie and the vegetables over the horse onto the road ahead of the mutilated possum. The wagon then turned on its left side, ejecting Will, who still clutched the reins.

"God damn it!" Will shouted. The front wagon wheel had come down on his right leg. He could see Buddy on his side snorting and called out for Willie. Where was that boy? Finally, Willie came limping over and started to cry as he saw Buddy on the ground and in pain.

"Willie, come here and listen to me!" shouted Will. "My leg is pinned under the wheel and it's hurt bad." He pointed to the soaked red spot on his overalls. "The wagon is too heavy for you to lift. Run down the road to the campground and bring back some men."

"What about Buddy?" Willie asked.

"Just go," Will yelled. He moaned. The last thing he saw before passing out were the buzzards circling overhead.

Chapter Two

HELL'S CAMPGROUND

WILL REGAINED CONSCIOUSNESS a few minutes later to intense pain and swelling in his right knee. He raised his head slightly and saw that the red stain on his overalls had gotten larger, and blood was running down his leg. Buddy was still snorting.

He remembered that he told Willie to run to the campground for help, but that was at least a mile away. How long would it take for help to arrive and remove the capsized wagon that pinned him? His stomach knotted, and his hands began to shake. Would it be in time to save his life?

As he drifted in and out of consciousness, he thought about Elizabeth and his daughters. How would they survive without him? Even if he was saved, how would he be able to take care of his farm with a bum leg? Why did Elizabeth make him take the vegetables to the religious nuts at the campground? It was all her God damned fault!

Then his thoughts turned to what Elizabeth would do if she were there with him. She was a comfort, always calming him down when his anger flared. He envisioned her by his side stroking his forehead and praying for his pain to go away.

For the first time since his father died, Will thought about praying. He didn't know how to do it, but in desperation gave it his best. "God, I don't know if you exist, but if you do, I need your help right now. Please don't let me down." He stopped suddenly, thinking this sounded stupid. "But you probably don't exist, so you can forget it if you want."

The next thing Will heard was the sound of galloping horses in the distance and then a great commotion of loud voices. Will was conscious, but Buddy was quiet now and looked like he had fallen asleep. Will raised up and saw Willie jump down from a bearded stranger's horse and run to Buddy. His son sobbed with relief when Buddy opened his eyes.

The bearded man came over to Will. "I'm Reverend Robert Todd from the camp meeting up the road. I'm sorry about your accident. Your son tells me you're Elizabeth Thompson's husband."

After unharnessing Buddy, Rev. Todd and three other men grunted and groaned as they lifted the wagon and its wheel from Will's right leg. Will tried to stand, but he couldn't bear his own weight on the injured leg and howled at the pain. Rev. Todd tried to console him. "I pray you'll be okay. We'll get you to a doctor to look at that leg."

Rev. Todd went over to check on Buddy, who was still being comforted by Willie. Will had seen other horses snorting with an injured leg, and his father had to put them out of their misery. "You're probably goin' to have to put him down," moaned Will. "My rifle should be under the wagon bench."

"Wait," Willie cried. "I think Buddy's going to be okay. It's just his front right knee is banged up a little."

Leaning against the wagon wheel that had pinned him minutes earlier, Will saw Rev. Todd move the horse's legs back and forth and up and down. Announcing that there didn't seem to be any broken bones, he focused on Buddy's injured knee, which had a small gash and some dried blood. Buddy craned his neck and tried to get up but could not move his weight forward.

"Let's help him get on his feet," Todd said to the other men. They slung a rope behind Buddy's hindquarters. As Willie and the bearded man pulled on Buddy's bridle, the other men yanked hard on the rope, and Buddy lunged forward into a standing position.

When the old horse took a few limping steps, Todd smiled and returned his attention to Will. "I see from what was spilled on the road that you were doing God's work by bringing us chickens and vegetables."

"I don't know about God's work," Will said. Why would a God cause all this to happen, he wondered. My only horse is hurt bad, and I don't know if I'll ever be able to walk right again.

"You have a good son," Rev. Todd said. "He kept your horse calm and came for help. Now, since it's getting late, I'm going to hitch my horse up to your wagon and bring you, your son, and your horse to the campground."

"Where will my son and I stay tonight?" Will asked.

"Mr. Thompson, you and your boy will be fine," Rev. Todd said. "We have plenty of food at the camp. I'll have Doc Marsh look at your leg and clean up your knee. You can sleep in my tent house, and you and your son can attend the evening service if you like."

Will knew he didn't have a choice. It was too late to get home before dark even if he borrowed a horse. Although he felt sick to his stomach, he suspected that Willie and Buddy needed to be fed.

As Rev. Todd gathered the spilled vegetables from the ground and placed them back in the baskets, the other three men lifted Will up to sit on the back of the wagon with his legs dangling. From his perch, Will noticed that the kettle with the chickens was on its side in the road, but somehow the lid had remained secured by the handle. Well, at least something went right, Will mused.

Rev. Todd hitched his horse to Will's wagon and climbed up into the seat, beckoning Willie to join him. Two of the other men jumped back on their horses, and the third began walking with his horse and Buddy, who was still limping, in tow.

Within 15 minutes, the group reached the Zoar Church and the adjacent oak grove where the camp meetings were held. Will was relieved to see Buddy had made it and was no longer snorting. Willie ran over to Buddy and stroked his forehead.

Will had been here before, but he had always dropped his

vegetables and chickens in the carriage lot next to the church. He had never seen inside the campground, but he had heard the preaching, singing, and wailing coming from the oak grove.

It was almost dusk when Rev. Todd helped Will down from the wagon, placing his left shoulder under Will's right armpit for support as they approached the campground with Willie trailing behind. They passed through a path in the large spreading oak trees.

Will could smell campfires burning and heard the happy voices of children playing. He saw small wood frame cottages and tents arranged in a circle around a large wooden structure with a shingled roof and benches. A piano and table with a wooden cross and large brass cup were placed in the front of the structure. There was a raised platform with steps for access. He guessed this was the tabernacle he heard Elizabeth go on about.

Typical Camp Meeting Tabernacle with Adjacent Tent-House (Clarksville, DE Camp, from *Cultivating the Methodist Garden, a brief history of the Peninsula-Delaware Conference of the United Methodist Church,* Barbara Duffin and Philip Lawton, 2000)

Rev. Todd led Will and Willie to a frame cottage right behind the front of the tabernacle. He ushered them in through a screen door and gently lowered Will onto a canvas cot. As he lit an oil lamp, Rev. Todd said, "You and your son can rest in my tent house, Mr. Thompson. I'll go find Doc Marsh."

The tent house had a wood plank floor and smelled musty like Will's root cellar at the farm. He looked around and saw two cots, a small bureau, a table, a wash stand with basin, and two dilapidated chairs. There was an old Bible, a stack of papers, and a quill pen and ink bottle on the table. Willie leafed through the Bible that was marked up with underlining and notes in the margins.

"Pop, do you think Buddy's going to be okay?" asked Willie.

Will tried to stand and fell back on the cot with a groan. "I sure hope so, son. We need him on the farm. I don't know how we'll get our vegetables and meats to the market in Lewes without Buddy."

"Then why'd you want to kill him?"

"I thought he had a broke leg. And horses can't live like that. I jus' wanted to put him out of his misery."

"I'm glad Reverend Todd saved him from what you wanted to do with your gun."

Will glared at his son and cleared his throat. Before he could say anything, Rev. Todd burst through the screen door with an older man behind him carrying a black bag. "This is Doc Marsh. We're blessed that he was here for tonight's service. You're in his good hands and the Lord's healing power. I need to get ready for the service." Rev. Todd quickly changed his shirt, put on a ribbon tie and bowler hat, and rushed out of the tent house.

"Pull your overalls down and let me have a look," the doctor said.

Will gingerly peeled back the denim from his blood-clotted knee. He unclasped the shoulder snaps and lowered his overalls over his old work shoes to the dirty wood plank floor of the tent house. The doctor squinted through his eyeglasses at the swollen knee and moved Will's lower right leg in all directions as he cried out in pain. "God damn, that hurts, Doc."

"It looks like you've torn something around the knee," said the doctor. "I'll clean up the wound and bandage it, but you'll need to keep off that leg for quite a while."

"Is it ever goin' to be right?" asked Will.

"Hard to say," the doctor answered. "If there's a tear, it eventually will heal, but you might need a brace to be able to walk on it and then with a limp. I saw a lot of these in the war."

The doctor cleaned the wound with water from the washbasin. He reached into his bag for iodine, which he applied to the gash on the side of Will's knee before wrapping it in a cotton bandage. "You need to watch this and make sure it doesn't get infected. If you get gangrene, your leg will have to come off above the knee."

Will's jaw dropped as the doctor opened the black bag again and pulled out a bottle of whiskey in a paper sack. "Drink a shot of this at least once an hour. It should help with the pain. And don't let Todd or anyone else here see that I gave this to you."

Grimacing, Will remembered Elizabeth saying these holy rollers were teetotalers. He shoved the bottle in the pocket of his overalls. "God damn it," he moaned.

"Pop, you know Mama doesn't—"

"Shut your mouth, son."

"Willie, open the screen door for me," said Rev. Todd as he came up to the tent house carrying two large plates brimming full of chicken, corn, tomatoes, and sweet potatoes. "I'll be right back with some apple pie, and then I have to preach."

"Pop, this smells just like Mama's cookin'. Reverend Todd sure is good to us."

Will nodded with a grunt. "That's his job, helpin' folks. But be careful, son, some things ain't always what they appear to be."

Rev. Todd returned in a flash with the pie. Willie had already finished his plate of food and thanked him as Todd dashed out. Will just stared at his plate without even tasting it. He was too upset and in too much pain to eat. He pulled the bottle out of his overalls and took a long swig.

Will could hear the piano start to play. After a few minutes, they heard Rev. Todd's voice booming from the tabernacle. "Friends, you may wonder why bad things happen to good people. Tonight, I am going to tell you why."

Will snickered at what he'd just heard. How does this preacher have all the answers?

Todd continued, "God doesn't want any of us to suffer, but we live in a broken world where Satan roams around looking to cause trouble. Why just tonight a fine man was bringing us food from his farm when his horse spooked and his wagon turned over on top of him. He's injured and in great pain. Even though you don't know him, please pray tonight for healing for Will Thompson and for his wife and children."

Will was surprised and embarrassed to hear these words. Was Todd going to make him the laughingstock of these religious fanatics? Frustrated that he was in no condition to do anything about it, Will took another big gulp of the whiskey and lay back on the cot as Rev. Todd continued with his sermon.

It was completely dark now. Will heard the crickets chirping and the cicadas buzzing in the trees nearby. As he drifted in and out of sleep, Todd quoted verses from his Bible and talked about some man named Job who suffered while trying to do good.

Will woke up as Todd was building to a thunderous climax. "God is in on the throne and ultimately in control of what happens to us. What may appear in this world to be the worst thing is never the last thing. Do I hear an amen to that?"

Those gathered in the tabernacle and some still in their tent houses shouted, "Amen, brother." From the cot beside Will, Willie joined them in this chorus, tears running down his cheeks.

The piano played Amazing Grace, and Rev. Todd invited those who had not yet accepted Jesus as their Lord and Savior to come to the altar. Willie ran from the tent house and joined a dozen men, women, and children kneeling at the table in the front of the tabernacle. Rev. Todd came to each of them, offering a prayer as he touched their shoulder.

After another verse of Amazing Grace, the service ended, and

Will saw his son talking with the young man who had played the piano. As sharp pain returned to his knee, Will took another swig of the whiskey and closed his eyes. He wondered if he had died and gone to Hell.

Reverend Robert Washington Todd (*circa* 1858, from Whatcoat U.M.C., Camden, DE website).

Chapter Three

HOMECOMING

WILL AWOKE WITH a start to thunder and lightning. It was still dark, and he heard heavy rain falling through the open window. As he bent his right knee, he felt excruciating pain. The whiskey's numbing effects had worn off. He looked over to the other cot and saw Willie sleeping soundly.

Realizing the prior day's events were not just a bad dream, Will reached for the bottle in his pocket and took another long swig. He thought of Elizabeth and knew she and his daughters would be distraught because he and Willie had not returned. Why had this terrible turn of events happened to him?

He tried to remember Rev. Todd's preaching. Something about why bad things happen even though God is in charge. He had seen some very bad things happen in the war. Where was God in all of that? Why did those young men wearing crosses and professing Jesus as their savior have to die such gruesome deaths? He took another big swallow of the whiskey, let out a groan, and drifted back into a deep sleep.

The sunrise brought light to the campground and through the window of the tent house. A rooster crowed, and Will opened one eye not knowing where he was at first. Suddenly, a bugle blasted out reveille, and he thought he was back at a battlefield encampment. As he tried to stand up and felt stabbing pain in his knee, the events of yesterday came flooding back. He quickly sat down and took another big gulp of whiskey, emptying the bottle.

The smell of bacon frying wafted through the open window. Will raised up and could see that the windowsill was wet from last night's rain, but the inside of the tent house was as dry as a bone. Will heard voices in the distance. There was a light knock at the screen door. It opened, and there stood Rev. Todd wearing the same clothes from last night. They were wet and caked with mud.

"How you feeling?" Rev. Todd whispered. "You getting hungry?"

"I'm makin' it," Will said. "Where'd you sleep last night?"

"We had an extra tent, so I camped out there. You must be starved. How 'bout some breakfast?"

Will had not eaten since noon the prior day and felt a gnawing in his gut. He wondered why this preacher had slept on the wet ground in a tent last night and given him and Willie his tent house. Todd must be crazy, he mused.

Willie rolled over and opened his eyes halfway. "Where are we, Pop?"

"It's okay, son. We'll be goin' home soon."

"Good morning, Willie," said Rev. Todd. "How about if you come with me to the boarding tent and help bring some breakfast back for you and your father."

"Son, hurry up and go with the preacher," Will said. "We need to be leavin' soon. Your mother and sisters must be worried sick about us not comin' home last night."

Willie jumped out of bed and followed Rev. Todd to the boarding house on the other side of the campground. They returned with two plates of bacon and eggs and a tin cup of coffee. With a moan, Will sat up on his cot and gobbled down his food.

He looked outside through the screen door and saw Rev. Todd standing there waiting for them to finish eating. "I need to check on Buddy and see if he's up to pulling the wagon home," he called to Todd.

The preacher nodded. "He's in the pen. You can take a look. I checked on him earlier this morning and fed him. He's still limping pretty bad and I don't think he'll be able to pull your wagon."

"You mean I can't even take my horse home? Jesus Christ! Why did Elizabeth send me to this God damn place to have all this trouble?"

Todd closed his eyes and took a deep breath. "You can borrow my horse, Gideon, and I'll have the vet come and take a look at Buddy's knee later today or tomorrow. You can have Gideon for as long as you need. I'm sure one of our campers has an extra horse I can use. Your son and I will get Gideon hitched up to your wagon, and we'll get you going."

Will tried to take in what he just heard. Was the reverend out of his mind? He suddenly felt a flash of shame for the language he had used.

Todd soon returned with another man, and together they helped Will to his feet. Todd put his shoulder under Will's right armpit, and they made their way slowly to the carriage lot next to the church. Along the way, Will saw families gathered around campfires praying together and reading from their Bibles. He heard them discussing last night's sermon.

As they reached the clearing, the sun was rising and a light breeze beckoned a beautiful late summer day. Carriages and farm wagons were arriving with families headed to the tabernacle. Will wondered how these farm folks had time for this.

Willie was waiting with a dark brown Arabian hitched up to their wagon. "This is Gideon," said Todd. "He's a hard worker and gentle."

The men lifted Will onto the seat of the wagon. He felt knife-stabbing pain as he bent his knee and nearly passed out. "Where's the Doc?" Will asked. "I might need some more of his medicine."

"He went home after last night's service," said Rev. Todd. "How about if I help you get back to your farm?"

Before Will could answer, Todd ran to the pen and brought another horse that he tied to the back of the wagon. He threw a saddle and harness into the wagon, telling Willie to sit in the back and keep an eye on it. With that, he jumped up on the wagon's bench next to Will, and they were off before Will could ask any more questions.

Todd clicked his tongue to get Gideon moving and yanked gently on the reins to keep him going at a slow pace as they pulled out on the bumpy road. Will stretched out his right leg and rested his shoe on the buckboard. That seemed to ease the pain, and he gave a sigh of relief.

As they rumbled down the road, Will noticed the sweet smell of honeysuckle. When he first met Elizabeth twenty years earlier, she had a sprig of honeysuckle in her beautiful long brown hair that fell gently onto her pink and white gingham dress. Will had been on his way home from delivering vegetables for his father when he happened to stop by the outdoor church bazaar in Lewes. He was only 17 but fell in love immediately with Elizabeth Maull, and they were married in less than a year. Life was so much simpler then, Will mused.

As they pulled off the road to Zoar onto the Millsboro Road to head east toward Rehoboth, Todd asked where Will's farm was located. "I've never been to Rehoboth or seen the sea," remarked Todd. "I'll bet it's a beautiful and plentiful place just like the Rehoboth in Genesis."

"I don't know about that," said Will. "We almost never get down to the ocean. Too much work to do on the farm, and I don't know how to swim anyhow. I sometimes go huntin' in the salt marshes."

Will's thoughts returned to his injured knee and limping horse and how his whole life had changed yesterday in an instant. "Reverend, I heard a little bit of your preachin' last night about why bad things happen to good people. How come God, iffn' there is such a thing, caused me all this trouble?"

"That's a good question. I don't believe that God wants or causes us to have troubles. Sometimes we bring it on ourselves and suffer the consequences of our poor choices. Other times, bad things happen because we live in a fallen world where the Evil One is at work and there's accidents, injuries and illness and nothing you can do to stop it."

"But I thought I heard you say God is in control. If he is, then why don't he just kill or stop the Evil One from causin' me trouble?" Will asked.

Todd paused as they turned onto the main road. He gave Gideon a snap with the reins to get him trotting. "Will, that's one of the great mysteries of our faith. It goes back to Adam and Eve in the Garden of Eden. But I can assure you that even in the midst of pain and suffering caused by our own actions or the Devil, God never leaves us alone if we let him into our hearts."

Will thought about what he'd just heard. "I guess I never let him in. Never needed to. I like to solve my own problems." He lowered his voice so Willie wouldn't hear. "But right now, I'm at the end of my rope."

"We've all been there, Will," said Rev. Todd.

Gideon was picking up speed now as they headed east into the morning sun and turned south toward Rehoboth. Will saw that Gideon was a much younger and stronger horse than Buddy. He wondered again why Todd would just give him this valuable work animal for as long as he needed it.

As they passed the corn and soybean fields glistening with last night's rain, Will dreamed of buying more land next to his small farm and growing these cash crops for harvest and sale. Selling vegetables in the summer and a few chickens year-round helped them get by, but he longed to own a larger and more productive farm so he could split it up for his children to live nearby and raise their own families. His brother would never sell any of his inherited land, but the farmer on the other side of Will's property was getting up there in years and had no children interested in farming.

Will began to feel a little more hopeful. His knee didn't hurt as much as it did last night. Maybe Gideon could fill in on the farm until Buddy recovered. He looked at Rev. Todd's muddy clothes and recalled that he and Willie had slept in his dry tent house while the preacher had endured the thunderstorm and torrential rain in a leaking tent. I guess I should be more grateful, he thought.

"Is this the way to your farm?" asked Rev. Todd as they approached Rehoboth. A long, tree-lined lane to a stately farmhouse came into view.

Will's father had left the family farm in Rehoboth Neck to George, the older son. That included three hundred acres of fertile farmland and pastures, the comfortable family homestead and outbuildings and a barn full of cows and horses. As the younger son, Will was bequeathed only a ten-acre plot with a small building that housed the family servants before the war.

"Naw, that's the lane to my brother's farm. My farm's a little further up."

"Looks like your brother has quite a few horses," Rev. Todd said as they passed a fenced pasture with more than a dozen horses grazing.

Will nodded, thinking his greedy brother wouldn't loan him a horse if his life depended on it.

Todd turned Gideon up the short lane, and Will's heart jumped when he saw Elizabeth hanging clothes on a line in front of the house. He realized how much he had missed her yesterday when he was lying in pain on the road and in the tent house last night.

She dropped her clothes basket and ran to meet the approaching wagon. "Praise the Lord, my prayers have been answered," Elizabeth exclaimed as she climbed up on the wagon and embraced first Will and then Willie. She called to the girls, who were feeding the pigs and chickens and picking the vegetables as Will always did in the morning. They came running to greet their father and younger brother.

It was a homecoming that touched Will's heart. He explained the events of the prior day and how Rev. Todd and others at the camp meeting had helped them. He told them that the Reverend had offered to loan them his horse until Buddy was better.

Rev. Todd jumped down and came alongside Elizabeth. "Thank you for the chickens you sent. Your husband's knee is hurt pretty bad. He needs to keep the wound clean and stay off the leg as much as possible so it can heal. I'll have Doc Marsh check on him in a few days. I have to get back to the campground, as I'm preaching this afternoon."

"I was going to bring the girls to the campground today," Elizabeth said, "but we need to look after Will and get the farm work done here." Will felt grateful to hear Elizabeth say that, because he needed her right now. "We might come over to Zoar later this week when things calm down," she added.

"If you make it, be sure to bring him," Rev. Todd said, motioning to Willie, who already was making friends with Gideon. Todd helped Will down from the wagon and walked him over to the front porch, where Will sat down with a grunt in an old wooden chair. The reverend reached his hand out to Will and said, "Mr. Thompson, I hope you'll come back to the campground when you feel up to it."

Will swallowed his pride and shook Todd's hand. "Thanks for your help. I probably wouldn't be here except for you."

Chapter Four

SALVATION

ELIZABETH SAT NEXT to Will on the porch and stroked his forehead with a damp cloth as he related the events of last 18 hours. "I'm really sorry I told you to hurry to the campground. I feel like it's all my fault."

"Of course it's not your fault," Will said, looking off into the distance at his small field of withering corn. "Sometimes stuff just happens. I'd have died on that road to Zoar if you hadn't suggested Willie go with me."

"Mary and Hannah," Elizabeth shouted to the twins inside the house, "please bring your father some ham, cheese, and hard tack. Ruth, please go to the well and get some fresh cold water."

The twins, wearing identical cotton dresses and bonnets, promptly appeared with the food.

"Poppa, are you in pain?" asked Hannah.

"I feel so bad for you," offered Mary.

"I'll be fine, girls," replied Will. "This banged up knee will heal in no time, Lord willing."

Elizabeth and the twins stared at Will, looking stunned.

"What's wrong?" asked Will. "You never heard me talk about the Lord?" He was surprised and a little embarrassed the word had come from his mouth. Was Rev. Todd rubbing off on him? Or was he just trying it on in front of his family to see what it felt like?

The older sister, Ruth, came running up with a full bucket of water that sloshed over the sides as she ran. She dipped a tin cup in it and held it to her father's lips. "Here, Poppa, hope this helps."

Willie returned from feeding Gideon and putting him in the fenced pasture behind the barn. "Pop, Gideon is a really good horse. We're lucky Reverend Todd let us borrow him."

"Yes, we are," Will said between bites of the hard tack that he had stacked with the ham and cheese. "That Reverend Todd is a good man." Will felt ashamed that he had misjudged the preacher and cursed in front of him. He hoped he could see him again and make amends.

Will finished eating, and the girls left to do their chores. Willie went inside and began playing the piano. "Elizabeth, we're blessed to have such carin' children. I've been takin' them and you for granted for too long. Maybe I should go to church with you and kids once in a while."

He didn't want to promise too much, but he knew what he said was important to Elizabeth.

Elizabeth patted Will on his good knee. "That would be good for all of us," she said with a smile.

The mid-day sun came over the house and heated up the porch like an oven. Elizabeth helped Will to his feet and steadied him as they went inside to their bed, where he lay down. She pulled the bandage back to look at his knee. A yellow discharge oozed from the wound. She mopped it with a cotton cloth as Will winced.

Will studied Elizabeth's face and movements. She looked weary but never complained about all the work she had to do on the farm while raising four children. He was lucky to have her as his partner. He could not do this alone.

"We should get the doctor to look at this," she said. Will nodded and dozed off to sleep.

When he woke up, Elizabeth was singing a hymn as she prepared dinner in the kitchen. He thought about his family and the choices he and Elizabeth had made. He wondered if they were the right ones. They had married when they were still in their teens.

Elizabeth's father had been a pilot boat captain on the Delaware Bay and River. Her mother had worked for the minister at Bethel Church, before their fishing boat capsized and they drowned in a freak storm in the Delaware Bay. Will, Elizabeth, and the children had lived with them in their large home on Pilottown Road in Lewes until the war ended, but Will wanted to show his father and brother he could make it on his own farming. He asked his father for his inheritance early, and he and Elizabeth moved into the deserted slave quarters, which he fixed up and added on to, and they began farming.

Ruth was now seventeen and becoming a beautiful young woman. Will watched as Elizabeth taught her to cook, wash clothes, and tend to the farm animals. Elizabeth had insisted that, just as she had done, Ruth would attend the one-room private grammar school near Lewes for six years where she learned to read, write, and do arithmetic. After that, Elizabeth took her to Sunday school at Bethel, where she read books, studied history, and learned to sing and write poetry. She would make some young farmer a helpful wife, Will mused, especially one like him who couldn't read or write.

He heard the twins laughing and playing checkers in the adjacent room. They were two years younger than Ruth and had benefitted greatly from their older sister's teaching. He was glad to see Elizabeth instruct them on what was expected of a farm wife.

The piano was playing, and Will thought about how Willie, at the age of two or three, watched his mother play and became captivated by its sound. After the twins were born, Will had longed for a son to carry on the Thompson name. Elizabeth became pregnant again, but they were devastated when they discovered the infant boy was a blue baby and died after three days. They buried "Baby Thompson" on the farm and had a crude headstone made by a local mason.

Then Will recalled how excited he was when Willie came along. He finally had a son who could help on the farm and inherit it one day. But would Willie even want that?

Elizabeth quietly pushed open the door to their tiny bedroom. "Doc Marsh is here. Are you up to seeing him?"

"Yes," answered Will, surprised that the doctor was back so soon. "I may need some medicine for this knee."

The doctor examined Will's knee and cleaned it again with iodine and a fresh bandage. "You need to have your wife use this on you at least twice a day," he said, putting a small bottle of the iodine on the old wooden bureau next to his bed. "How's the pain?"

"Not too bad right now. But I might need some more of that strong pain killer you gave me last night. How come you're back so soon?"

"Reverend Todd told me you needed looking after and gave me a little something for my time," Doc Marsh said, looking over his wire-rimmed glasses. "I don't have any more of that pain killer right now," he added in a low voice. "And I'd recommend you not get depending on it."

Will understood. He'd had a big problem with alcohol during the war when he and his brother, like most of the others in their company, drank way too much whiskey and malt. They would start drinking in the morning and be three sheets to the wind most evenings. He took Elizabeth's stern demands to give up the bottle to heart after he returned home.

After the doctor left, Will slipped into a deep sleep. The next thing he knew it was morning and he could hear Elizabeth directing the children to do his early morning chores and prepare the wagon to go to the camp meeting. Will could not recall when he had slept that long and felt frustrated that his family was having to do his work.

Elizabeth brought a bowl of creamed dry beef into the bedroom. There was a side of toast and his tin cup was filled with steaming coffee. It was one of his favorite meals.

"The children and I are fixing to take Gideon and the wagon to Zoar," said Elizabeth. "Are you going to be okay here alone for a few hours? I could leave Willie or one of the girls to look after you."

"Oh, no. I'll be fine." Will sat up on edge of the bed to eat. "I might even go with you if my knee ain't too bad this mornin'." He couldn't help but notice Elizabeth's eyes open wider as she uttered a surprised "huh."

Elizabeth told Willie to hitch up Gideon to the wagon and asked his sisters to pick fresh vegetables to take to the camp meeting. Elizabeth returned to the bedroom to bid Will goodbye and found him standing next to the bed, dressed and with his shoes on.

"Will, you really don't need to go," said Elizabeth. "We're just going to attend the afternoon service and will be back before dark."

"Well, I've been doin' a lot of thinkin', and maybe there's a reason the wagon turned over and hurt my leg. I want to go back and let Reverend Todd know how much I appreciated his sendin' Doc Marsh to see me again. 'Sides, maybe Buddy's better and we can let him have his horse back."

With the help of a bushel basket for a stool, Elizabeth, Willie, and Ruth helped get Will up into the wagon. He sat on the bench up front with Elizabeth and the children rode in the back. The mid-morning air was still cool, and when they came to the fragrant honeysuckle patch, Will smiled and related his memory of their meeting to Elizabeth.

"That was a long time ago," said Elizabeth. "A lot's happened to us since those easy days. But God has been good."

Gideon was responsive to Will's urgings with the reins, and they made it to the campground in half the time it would have taken Buddy. As Will and his family entered the oak grove, passing by men guarding the perimeter, he was limping and using a cane Willie had made from a fallen tree limb. Will spotted Rev. Todd praying with a family in front of their tent house. Todd saw him and came over grinning with an outstretched hand.

"It's a blessing to see you, Will. How are you feeling?"

For the first time, Will looked the preacher in the eye. "Much better, Reverend Todd. And thanks for sendin' Doc Marsh to check on me. Didn't 'spect him so soon, and I know he don't work for free. How much do I owe you?"

"Don't worry about that," said Todd. "I'm glad your knee is healing. I wish I could say the same for Buddy. The vet was here this morning. Said it's going to be weeks or maybe months before Buddy's ready to pull a wagon. You need to hang on to Gideon for a while longer. Help yourself to some vittles in the boarding tent."

The preacher hurried off to his tent house, and Will and his family headed for the boarding tent to deliver the vegetables. After a filling lunch of chicken and dumplings, they found seats in the first row of the tabernacle as the piano began to play. The exhorters encouraged the gathered campers to prepare their hearts for the service, and then Rev. Todd appeared in his suit that still showed the mud stains from the storm two nights earlier.

After several hymns and a scripture reading from Exodus about the First Commandment, Will listened with an ear turned to the raised platform as Rev. Todd began to preach with a Bible clutched in his outstretched arm. "Just as God told Moses and the Israelites to have no other gods before Him, we are taught by Jesus to love God with all of our heart, soul, mind, and strength."

Many of the worshippers in the tabernacle and on the porches of their tent houses shouted a resounding "Amen, brother." Elizabeth nodded, and the children were also paying close attention.

Todd went on, raising his voice for emphasis. "That means we don't put our other gods—our own desires and interests—before serving God. It doesn't matter to God who has the biggest farm or the most money or the best horse. God looks at the heart of a man to see what he loves most. Our actions that demonstrate love to others is what He's most interested in."

This concept was brand new to Will. He always thought working hard and providing for his family was the most important thing. And if he could look a little more well off than his neighbors or his brother, that was even better.

Then it dawned on Will that Rev. Todd was talking about what he had just experienced. His heart jumped as he realized the events of the last two days had changed him. Was what he had seen as trouble really God trying to get his attention?

Will joined the others shouting, "Amen."

Elizabeth turned and hugged him. "I love you, Will Thompson," she whispered in his ear.

Will thought about how lucky he was to have a dedicated and loving wife like Elizabeth and four healthy children. He felt the light breeze caressing his cheek and listened to the rustling oak leaves. It was like a balm to his soul.

Before he knew it, the sermon ended and Will came forward to the simple altar, where he kneeled with some pain as Rev. Todd baptized him and gave him communion. Todd helped Will to his feet, and he returned to the wooden bench with tears in his eyes. He noticed that Elizabeth had been crying beneath her wide smile. He saw stunned looks on the children's faces and realized they had never seen their father in this condition.

After more singing and a closing prayer, the service ended, and Rev. Todd came over to Will. He threw his left arm over Will's shoulder and extended his right hand. Will grasped the preacher's hand and looked deeply into his eyes.

"Mr. Will Thompson, welcome to the family of God. I believe our Lord has much more in store for you."

Chapter Five

SHOTGUN GREETING

September 1872

"WE NEVER COULD'VE got this far on this new church building for Bethel without your skill at carpentry," Rev. Warner said as he shook Will's hand at the end of the worship service. They stood by the altar as the preacher offered Will the worn wicker collection basket. "Would you mind counting how much we collected this morning?"

"Thanks. I'd be happy to, Reverend." Will took the basket and looked up and admired the large oak beams in the ceiling and the raised altar. He felt proud that he was able to contribute his woodworking know-how to help build the new Methodist church in downtown Lewes. There was still a lot of work to be done to build out all of the Sunday school rooms and put the finishing touches on the spacious sanctuary, but Will felt confident he could get it done in the winter when he wasn't as busy on his farm.

As he counted the money, Will thought about how his work on the Bethel church construction led him to meet Elijah Miller, a young colored man from Pilottown whose father was the pastor of the St. George African Methodist Episcopal church on Pilottown Road. Elijah was paid ten cents per day as he worked for ten hours every Saturday that summer hauling up materials with a rope and pully and nailing the rafters and roof shingles on the church, something Will couldn't do with his bad leg. Working together, Will got to know Elijah and was impressed with his work ethic and friendly, positive attitude. He wondered how a Negro could be so happy.

Will watched his family heading out of the sanctuary to one of the Sunday school rooms. He emptied the handful of coins and a few bills from the basket onto the sturdy altar he had crafted from the finest hickory on his farm. Ever since he'd met Rev. Todd, Will's family had been coming to Bethel in its old one-room building at least twice a week.

It had been the best year of Will's life. Not only had he broadened his knowledge about God as he listened to Rev. Warner and Elizabeth read from the Bible, but he also was attending Sunday school and, with Elizabeth's help, learning how to read and write. He always thought reading was something he didn't need to earn his living on the farm, but now he was seeing how it opened his mind to new ways of thinking.

As Will counted the offering using his fingers on both hands, he regretted not being able to give more. "I get sixteen dollars and thirty cents," he reported to Rev. Warner, who was wiping down the silver chalice and gathering the unused communion bread.

"That will help feed some of our needy." Rev. Warner put the money in a small wool sack. "Will, I've been meaning to tell you that Reverend Todd is coming down from Wilmington next month. He says in his letter that he knows you."

Will's heart skipped a beat as he recalled his encounter with Todd more than a year ago, a meeting that changed his life. "I missed seein' him at Zoar this summer. Is he doin' all right?"

"I saw him at the conference meeting in March. He was having trouble breathing and seemed depressed. He wrote me that he went to the camp meeting last month in Ocean Grove, New Jersey. Said the salt air was good for his health and his soul."

"Why's he comin' to Lewes?" asked Will. He longed to see Rev. Todd again and tell him about the changes in his life. He also wanted to pay him for Gideon, who had become part of the Thompson family ever since they had to put Buddy down last spring.

The preacher paused and looked around to see if anyone else was listening. "Reverend Todd says he wants to buy some land along the seashore where he can establish a camp meeting for his congregation in Wilmington."

"That would be amazing." Will thought about how many people could gather for worship and enjoy the sea breezes and fresh air. Zoar had been all right as a campground, but it was inland and very hot and sticky on most August days.

"I've been telling him about some land on the ocean a little north of Rehoboth Bay," Warner said in a low voice, gesturing toward Rehoboth. "Todd said he had a dream about such a place with sand dunes. He and some others from his congregation plan to come south on the train next month and have asked me to take them to inspect the land."

"I think I know the exact place you're talkin' about," said Will. "It's very close to my farm. Could I go with you when you show it to them?"

"I'm sure that would be fine. If they like it, you may be able to introduce them to the landowners and see if they'd be willing to sell them some ground."

Will rushed off to the adult Sunday school class, where he joined Elizabeth. He couldn't wait to tell her the good news about Todd coming to visit. It would be exciting to have a camp meeting ground like Zoar right in his backyard.

Two weeks later, Rev. Todd, along with three other ministers and a lawyer, arrived in Lewes. Rev. Warner and Will met them at the railroad station just before noon. As the train pulled into the new station with its brakes screeching, Will could smell the acrid odor of the coal being burned to power the steam locomotive. Local men first unloaded the leather mail pouch, followed by tools and clothing made in Wilmington. Local passengers waiting to board stood on the platform chatting, smoking, and reading the *Breakwater Light* newspaper.

Will spotted Rev. Todd wearing his preaching suit on the platform and quickly limped over to shake his hand. The reverend grinned broadly and threw his arm around Will's shoulder. "It's so good to see you, Will. I'm pleased to hear from Reverend Warner what a faithful servant you've become to Bethel."

Will was surprised to hear that Rev. Warner had been singing his praises. "Reverend Warner and Bethel have been good to me," he said. As Warner greeted Todd's traveling companions, Will took Todd to see Gideon, who was tied to a hitching post nearby.

"I see you and Willie have been taking good care of Gideon," Rev. Todd said. "Has he been behaving?"

"Yes, indeed. I couldn't ask for a better animal. I think of you every time he pulls our wagon or plows the fields. We lost Buddy a few months ago, and Willie was so upset. I don't know what we would've done without Gideon. I'd like to buy him from you. Make it official."

"We can figure all that out later," Todd said as he climbed up, panting and wheezing, into one of the two carriages Rev. Warner had arranged to take the group to Rehoboth. "We have more important business to take care of right now. How's your knee doing?"

"Much better than the last time you saw me. But I still got this limp."

"I see that. Would you care to ride with us?" Todd asked, gesturing to Rev. Warner and a Mr. Records, who he said was an attorney from Lewes.

Will gingerly climbed in and sat next to Todd, who was talking excitedly to Rev. Warner about seeing Rehoboth as they headed south on the wide dirt road. It was the perfect early autumn day. The cloudless sky was azure blue, and the air was crisp and clean. They passed fields of corn and wheat that local farmers were harvesting using mule-drawn threshers. At Midway, Rev. Todd asked Will about the chapel that stood out among the small hamlet of homes.

"That's connected with the Presbyterian Church in Lewes," Will explained. "We're about halfway to Rehoboth." He pointed to his right. "Over there is the road that goes to Zoar."

He paused, recalling that awful day on the road to Zoar. He and Willie could have died on that road. He mused that he was a much different kind of man then and wanted to focus on the present.

"Do you know why they call it Rehoboth?" Will asked Rev. Todd.

"Yes, in fact I do." Todd pulled a worn Bible out of his burlap travel bag and wetted his finger with his tongue to turn the pages. "Right here, in the twenty-second chapter of Genesis, we are told of the Valley of Gerar in Israel where Isaac settled with his tribe."

Will squinted to see the small print that Todd was reading.

Todd continued. "They dug a well, and Isaac named the place Rehoboth because the Lord had given them enough room to flourish and live in peace. You see, Rehoboth in Hebrew means 'room enough'."

"So how did Rehoboth get named after a place in Israel?" asked Will.

Todd pulled a handkerchief out of his suit pocket and blew long and hard to try and clear his nose. "This hay fever has me all clogged up," he said as he neatly folded the handkerchief and placed it back in his suit pocket. "I read that the word 'Rehoboth' came to America when our English forefathers discovered Rehoboth Bay two hundred years ago. They saw it was a broad bay with enough room to settle and flourish."

Will nodded. As they continued past Midway, the carriage picked up speed. Dust from the road clouded the open carriage. "What land are you lookin' at in Rehoboth?" asked Will.

Rev. Warner motioned to Mr. Records. "Our lawyer has researched the land records in Georgetown and can tell you."

"There are two parcels of approximately 200 acres each that run down to the ocean," said the attorney, unrolling a map to show Will. "One is owned by a Mr. Lorenzo Dow Martin, and the other by a Mr. John Marsh. Do you know them?"

Will smiled. "I sure do. Mr. Martin owns the farm just down the road from mine." As a boy, he had gone to hog killings at Martin's farm, and his father and Martin had hunted together. They'd been good friends. "I'm surprised he wants to sell his farm."

Rev. Todd raised his eyebrows and gestured for Will to continue as he pulled out his handkerchief and covered his nose and mouth.

"Mr. Marsh is part of the Marsh family that owned hundreds of acres on the north side of Rehoboth Neck," Will said, "includin' the old Peter Marsh house called the Homestead. I've seen him at the markets in Lewes."

Will had always hoped he could buy a piece of land from Lorenzo Dow Martin to enlarge his own farm, but he'd been put off by his neighbor every time he asked. "Has anyone talked to Mr. Martin?"

"Not really," said Todd. "We first need to see if their land is suitable for camp meeting purposes. Reverend Warner seems to think so."

Rev. Warner nodded enthusiastically. "I've been to lots of camp meetings. The land in Rehoboth is ideal for the purpose of bringing folks to Christ. There's a perfect oak grove, fresh water lakes, and the health-reviving seashore."

The carriages soon passed Will's small property before arriving at Martin's farm. Will was embarrassed at the modest size of his farm and didn't point it out until Rev. Todd asked him if that was where he had taken Will after his accident near Zoar.

"Yes. That's where my wife Elizabeth nursed me back to good health."

Once in Rehoboth, the men jumped down from the carriages and set out on foot to examine the properties. Will tried to keep up with Todd, who, despite his breathing difficulty, was almost running across the meadow toward the ocean. Will saw Martin's farmhouse on the right before they reached the dunes and a sandy beach.

"This is just as it appeared in my dream," said Todd as he turned in a circle. He kicked the sand with his shoe and reached down with his hand to examine its texture. "It's even better than Ocean Grove. You could pull a carriage on this sand, and there's enough room in the fields for streets, cottages, hotels, boarding houses, and a boardwalk."

The attorney held up the map for all to see, and Todd paced off where the metes and bounds of each of the 200-acre parcels appeared to be located. He stuck a wooden stake in each corner. The land owned by Marsh was almost entirely forested with mature pine trees, while Martin's property was an open meadow where some land had been tilled to raise crops. Small pines had been planted in rows on the lake's shore. Will told the men he thought the lake was about ten acres.

Rev. Todd approached the shore of the lake, scooped up a handful of water, and drank it. "Praise God! Delicious fresh water within a hundred yards of the ocean." A large-mouth bass jumped high out of the water. "Great fishing, too."

As they returned to the carriages, they discovered a dense grove of mature oak trees with very little underbrush on the highest ground set back almost a mile from the beach. "This is the perfect place for a tabernacle," declared Todd. Will saw the preacher raise his arms and almost dance with excitement.

The men gathered in a circle and bowed their heads to pray over the land. Just as Rev. Todd began, they were interrupted by a bearded man in overalls pointing a shotgun at them. "You's trespassin' on my land!" he shouted. "Who are you? What do you want?"

Will raised his head and recognized Lorenzo Dow Martin. "Mr. Martin, it's Will Thompson. These are my friends from Bethel Church in Lewes. We're looking at this area to possibly start a camp meeting. Could we talk to you about it?"

"I ain't interested in talkin' 'bout any camp meetin'. And I sure ain't interested in givin' up any of my land for holy rollers makin' a lot a noise. And Will Thompson, what are you doin' with these preachers? Your father and you never darkened the door of a church. You tryin' to make a buck? Take your new friends and go find some other land in Lewes before I has to use this shotgun."

Chapter Six

THE MARTINS' CONCESSION

THE PREACHERS, LAWYER, and Will ran. They jumped into the carriages and headed to Lewes without looking back. Will was confused by their encounter with Lorenzo Dow Martin until he recalled that Martin was a Presbyterian and had been acting rather eccentric lately.

Rev. Todd was breathing hard through his mouth and stroking his beard vigorously in the carriage across from Will. Will studied his face and could see the sadness in the reverend's eyes. He recalled how Todd had brought him comfort at Zoar a year earlier.

"Sorry you came all the way from Wilmington to almost get killed," Rev. Warner said to Todd, his voice trembling. "What's wrong with that man?"

"I don't think that's the end of our talkin' with Mr. Martin," Will said. "He don't understand our camp meetings. Let me talk with him in a few days."

"I hope you can make some headway," said Rev. Todd.

The carriages picked up speed as they retraced their route to Lewes. Will hadn't eaten any lunch, but his stomach was in knots from their encounter with Martin.

"Will, we really need Martin's land if my vision to build a Christian seaside resort like Ocean Grove is to be realized," said Todd, his voice breaking with emotion. "Even if Mr. Marsh is willing to sell, his two hundred acres is all wooded and would be too small and expensive to lay out streets and bring the railroad through. We need both parcels."

"I'm pretty sure the Marsh property can be had for the right price," Rev. Warner piped in. "I talked to John Marsh at the Lewes farmers market this summer, and he seemed interested. If we can get a breakthrough with Martin, I'll contact Mr. Marsh."

"How much would you have to pay for Mr. Martin's property?" Will asked.

"I'm not sure exactly," replied Todd. "I hope we can raise ten to fifteen thousand dollars for the whole venture, but we'll need to use most of that to build a tabernacle, hotel and other improvements."

"Do you have two thousand dollars for Mr. Martin's two hundred acres?" Will asked. "That's ten dollars an acre, which should be the goin' rate for farmland in this area."

"I think we can probably afford that," said Todd. "Maybe a

little more if it's needed. He could keep living in his farmhouse and we can give him a nice lot."

They reached Lewes as the afternoon sun was falling fast and the merchants were closing their shops. The rank smell of decaying fish permeated the air as the menhaden boats unloaded their catches. Rev. Warner invited the men from Wilmington to his home for dinner and to spend the night. Will hurried to find Gideon and ride back to his farm before dark.

THREE DAYS LATER, Will paid a visit to Lorenzo Dow Martin. It was early in the morning and raining hard, so Will figured that a busy farmer like Martin would be more amenable to taking time to talk. When the rain slowed, Will put on his ten-gallon hat, jumped on Gideon, and urged him to gallop through the puddles to the Martin farm. Will saw Martin feeding his hogs and joined him at the pen.

"Good morning, Will Thompson. Hope you're not coming here 'bout that Methodist camp meetin' foolishness."

"Do you know what they want to do on your land?"

"No, but I don't want any damn camp meetin' interfering with my plans."

"What do ya mean?"

"Well, have you thought about what happens to our land if they extend the railroad from Lewes to here?"

"You think that's goin' to happen any time soon?"

"I hear talk. And when the railroad gets here from Lewes, my land will be worth thousands of dollars to develop as a resort town like Ocean City is doin'."

Will paused to take that in. Maybe he could figure out a way to help Martin and Todd both get what they wanted. They walked up to Martin's farmhouse as the rain got heavier and sat down on two old rockers on the front porch.

"Mr. Martin, how are you goin' to get approval from the legislature to create a town and then afford to put in streets and other improvements?"

"Well, boy, as your pop used to say, we'll just see 'bout that."

"My pop and you did a lot of huntin' together, didn't ya?"

"Yup," replied Martin. "Your pop was a good man. I miss him."

"Did you and Pop ever shoot at the same deer and not know whose shot took it down?"

"I'm sure we did, son. Why'd ya ask?"

"Who got the money for sellin' the deer meat?"

Martin pulled on his beard as he thought. "We would've split it and stayed friends."

"I thought so," Will said. "What if the Methodists shot the deer and still gave you half of the money?"

"Are you plumb crazy, boy? What are you talkin' 'bout?"

Will explained to Martin about Todd's vision for the town. "Reverend Todd has the financial backers and lawyers to get the approvals to lay out streets and sell lots through the legislature. And they don't need to wait for the railroad to come, which may never happen."

"You sayin' I wouldn't have to hire lawyers and surveyors and oversee all the work?" Martin raised an eyebrow and squinted at Will with the other eye.

"That's right. You might even be able to stay in this house till you're ready to build a new house and retire from farmin' with all the money you'll get."

"How much is Todd willin' to pay?"

Will hesitated. He didn't want to play Rev. Todd's hand too soon. He stood up, removed his hat, and scratched his head. "I don't really know, but I'd guess as much as ten dollars an acre."

"It's worth a lot more than that," said Martin. "Let me talk to my wife and sleep on all this. You come by tomorrow morning at eight sharp, and we'll talk some more."

WILL RETURNED ON Gideon the next morning to find Mr. Martin sitting on the front porch waiting for him. Martin greeted Will with a warm handshake. Through the screen door, Will heard an organ playing a familiar hymn in the house.

"Kitty, he's here!" Martin shouted through the screen door.

Lorenzo Dow Martin Farmhouse (undated, courtesy of Delaware Public Archives).

The organ music stopped, and Mrs. Martin pushed open the door wearing a colorful church dress and a large hat. "Well, if it isn't George Thompson's little boy Will all growed up. I haven't seen you since you come here for hog killins with your family. Would you like some coffee?"

"Thank you, ma'am, but I'm fine." Will was surprised at their warm welcome.

"Let me not beat around the bush," said Mr. Martin. "I need to take my wife up to the Presbyterian church." He rose from his chair to look directly into Will's eyes. "I might be interested in selling my valuable land, but the price has to be right, and we want this farmhouse to stay here."

"I think that can be worked out." Will stared back into Martin's eyes.

"I don't want a penny less than five thousand, and I want a nice lot on the main street where we can build a new house."

Mrs. Martin, sitting in the other creaking rocker, smiled and nodded.

Will tried not to appear too excited. "I'll have to see if Todd can come up with that much. They also need John Marsh's land to make this work."

"I'll speak with John," offered Martin. "I believe he'll sell for the right price. I thought you wanted to buy a piece of my land, Will Thompson."

"I did at one time," said Will. "But a lot's changed in my life in the last year. I think a camp meetin' resort would be a good use of your land."

Will walked gingerly down the steps of the porch.

"I see you're limping," Martin said. "What happened?"

Will looked over his shoulder as he prepared to mount Gideon. "My wagon turned over a year ago, and I got pinned under the wheel. It's probably the best thing that could've happened to me."

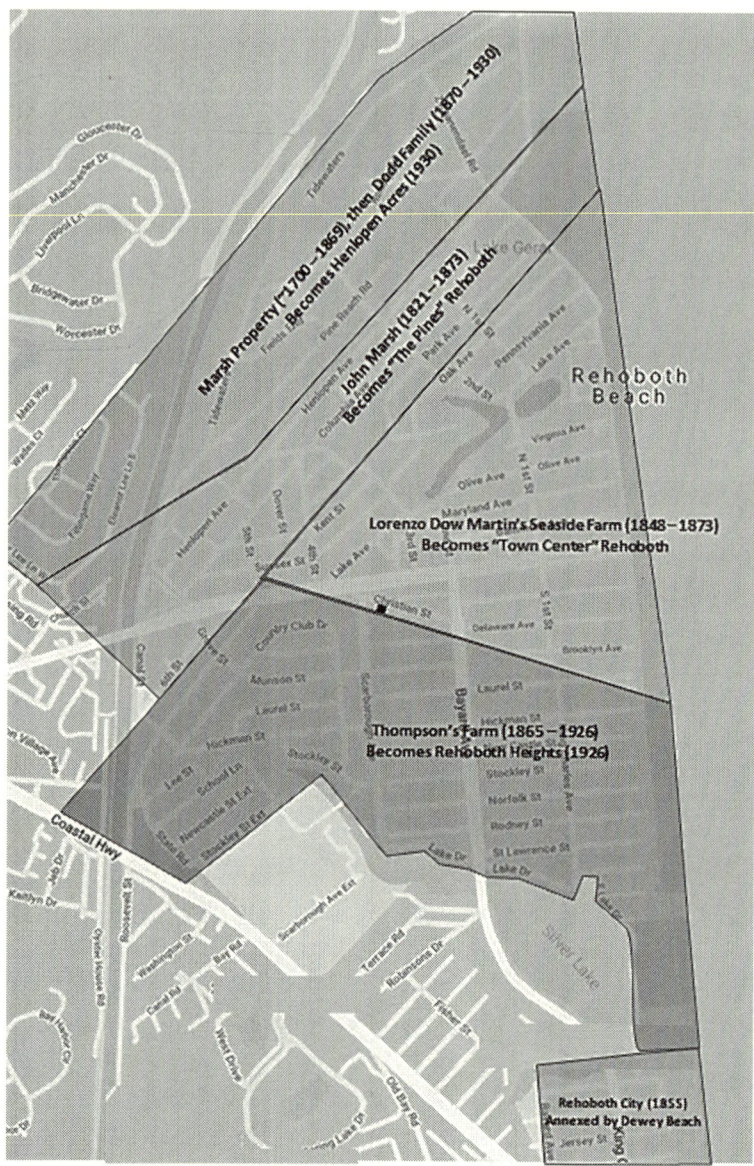

Land Ownership in Rehoboth Neck just prior to Rehoboth Beach Camp Meeting Association's purchases from Martin and Marsh in 1872-73 (annotated map courtesy of Paul Lovett).

Chapter Seven

ELIJAH

April 1873

WILL WOKE UP before dawn. He had barely slept. His heart raced as he thought about Rev. Todd coming to inspect the Rehoboth camp meeting grounds now under construction. He hadn't seen the preacher since October, when Martin had threatened them with his shotgun.

After a church service in January, Rev. Warner told Will that Martin and Marsh had sold their land to Rev. Todd's group. The camp meeting project in Rehoboth was full steam ahead. However, he gave Will no details other than Rev. Todd had asked if Will would keep an eye on the construction. Will readily agreed, and kept Rev. Warner updated each Sunday.

Will quickly fed Gideon, his pigs and chickens, milked the cow, loaded the wagon with his carpentry tools, and hitched

Gideon up to the wagon just as the sun was coming up. Elijah, the young Negro man from Pilottown who Will met last summer building the new Bethel Church, and who was helping to build the tabernacle, promised Will he would come to work early. There was much to do before the preacher arrived.

As Will returned to the farmhouse, he was surprised to see Elizabeth already up fixing him a hearty breakfast of ham and eggs. "Will Thompson, I've never seen you so excited," she said with a wide smile. "Tell Reverend Todd I'm praying for the camp meeting in Rehoboth this summer."

Will nodded as he wolfed down half of the breakfast while still standing in the kitchen. "Honey, could you please put the rest of this in a sack so I can take it for Elijah?"

"Go ahead and finish your breakfast." Elizabeth handed him a warm pot that he opened to find another serving of ham and eggs. "That's for Elijah. I put the rest of the fried chicken from last night's dinner in there for your lunch and there's enough for Elijah and Reverend Todd too."

"Thank you, Elizabeth." Will thought about how she had encouraged him to help Rev. Todd build the campground and had taken up the slack of farm work he no longer had time to do. He heard the mourning doves cooing and realized how much richer his life was than two years before. "You're a good woman, Elizabeth. And the best wife a man could ask for."

She smiled and her eyes looked wet. Will took out his handkerchief and dabbed her cheek. "The first camp meetin' is in July, and there's still a lot of work left to do."

"I'm sure Reverend Todd will be pleased with the progress on the tabernacle. I'm so proud of you."

"Reverend Todd won't get here till early afternoon. It'll be late when I get back." Will finished eating and headed for the front door.

"That's fine," said Elizabeth, following him. He turned, and she embraced him and kissed him deeply on the lips.

WHEN WILL GOT to the camp ground, Elijah Miller was already working on the roof beams of the tabernacle. Elijah, in his early twenties and strong, had been helping build the tabernacle on Saturdays for the past six weeks and never asked Will for a nickel. They had become friends as they toiled together, lifting the heavy lumber and nailing it into place.

Elijah was the first Negro man Will had gotten to know. They shared stories about their families and their faith. Elijah explained how Negroes were mistreated before, during and after the war, and that he didn't trust white men, especially ones who wouldn't even acknowledge his presence unless he was in the wrong place.

Will considered what it would've been like if he had been born black. What would being a person viewed as inferior have felt like? How would his family life have been different? Would he, like Elijah, know the Bible scriptures and pray every chance he got? Will wondered if he would ever become such a faithful Christian.

"Elijah, you're up early!" Will shouted up to the roof. Elijah was already glistening with sweat on the warm Saturday morning that was unusually humid for this time of year. The clouds were moving fast, and the boughs of the large oaks were starting to sway.

During their time together, Will learned that Elijah's family had been freed by a Methodist plantation owner in North Carolina after President Lincoln emancipated the slaves. They ended up on the poor side of Lewes as sharecroppers when Elijah was only 14 years old, the same age as Willie.

"I hope to meet Reverend Todd when he gets here cause I got something to ask him," Elijah yelled back.

Elijah had related to Will that his father was a minister with the small African Methodist Episcopal church on Pilottown Road in Lewes, and their congregation hoped to use the tabernacle when it was available. He guessed that was what Elijah wanted to talk to Rev. Todd about.

"Elijah, come on down here. My wife made you some breakfast."

Elijah slid down one of the oak columns supporting the rafters. He sat down on one of the benches Will had built for the tabernacle. "You got a good wife, Mister Thompson," remarked Elijah as he pulled a small book from the pocket of his denim work pants.

"You're right about that, Elijah. Just call me Will."

Elijah opened the well-worn book and read a short prayer of thanksgiving.

"How did you learn to read?" Will asked.

"We worked hard six days on the plantation. We rested on the Sabbath and went to Sunday school. That's where the master's daughter taught us to read and about Jesus. That's how my daddy become a preacher."

"I feel like we are brothers in Christ."

"Do you have any blood brothers, Mister Will?"

Will studied Elijah's interested face and realized he could not dodge the question. There was a distant rumble, and both men looked to the sky.

"I do have one, but we're not close. He don't believe in God and has too much land and money to feel any need to."

"I feel sorry for him. My family's poor but not in spirit."

"You said your father's a preacher and wants to use the tabernacle for worship services when it's done?" Will asked.

"Some of our congregation might even want to hear Reverend Todd preach the word if that would be all right."

"I'll ask him. I think I saw some colored folks sitting behind the preacher at the tabernacle at Zoar." Elijah had told him his family traveled on the Underground Railroad to Philadelphia to escape being captured by the bounty hunters hired by other plantation owners. "Aren't you afraid that some of the whites might not like that?"

"No, sir. My daddy taught me that there will be trouble for us in this life but not to be 'fraid of what happens to us cause the best is yet to come in the next life with Jesus."

Thunder rumbled closer. The sky was getting darker, and it smelled like rain. "Elijah, you need to hurry and finish up the roof beams. I'll be back to help in a few minutes. I want to take a look at how the grading of Rehoboth Avenue is coming along. I got some tools in the wagon for you."

Elijah hurried to the wagon, grabbed a large metal hammer, and climbed back up the column to work on the rafters. With his bad knee, Will realized he couldn't have built the tabernacle's rafters without Elijah.

Will walked toward the ocean on the new dirt road under construction. He could smell the salt air and passed the front porch of the Martins' farmhouse. It was hard to believe this was just a dream a year ago. He felt grateful that his meetings with the Martins had yielded fruit for Rev. Todd.

When he was halfway to the beach, Will saw two mule-driven graders smoothing out and compacting the dirt for the wide boulevard that would be called Rehoboth Avenue. One of the men operating the bladed graders was Lorenzo Dow Martin. Will went over to him.

"Mr. Martin, I'm surprised to see you here."

"Why's that? The quicker we can git this town built, the sooner I can build a new home for me and Kitty. Anyways, I git some of my money in installments as the town develops."

"Well, thanks for helping. Reverend Todd's comin' later today to check on our progress."

A loud clap of thunder and bolt of lightning struck nearby, causing Martin and Will to jump.

"That looked like it hit back by the oak grove," said Mr. Martin, shaking from the close call. "You might want to see if everything's okay."

Will limped in a hurry back to the tabernacle as rain began to fall. There were more claps of thunder, and the rain was coming down in sheets. As he reached the tabernacle, he was soaked to the bone and didn't see Elijah working on the rafters.

Will's heart raced, and his throat tightened. Then he saw Elijah lying on the ground in the tabernacle with Will's hammer still clutched in his hand. Will rushed over, shouting, "Elijah, are you all right?" There was no answer.

Elijah's shoes had been blown off his feet, and his eyebrows and hair were singed. There was scarring on his back and he wasn't breathing. Will felt helpless as he put his ear to Elijah's chest and could not hear his heart beating.

He cried out, "God, how could you let this happen to this good man who was buildin' your temple?"

There was no answer.

Chapter Eight

JOURNEY TO PILOTTOWN

WILL SAT DOWN on the tabernacle bench next to Elijah's lifeless body and wept. Why would God let this happen? To Elijah in the prime of life? At this place? Right now?

Was it his fault? He had encouraged his friend to hurry and finish the rafters before Rev. Todd arrived. Was it his metal tool that had attracted the lightning bolt?

The rain stopped, and the storm moved on. Will watched Elijah's face, which seemed calm and almost smiling. Maybe he knew it was his time? Maybe he was right, and the best was yet to come?

Will pondered what to do next. It would be several hours before Rev. Todd arrived. He needed to get Elijah back to his family in Lewes. They needed to know. How could he do that alone?

Then he remembered Lorenzo Dow Martin and found himself limping back toward the ocean. He blamed himself for convincing Martin to sell his land.

Will found Martin and his wife at their farmhouse and explained what had happened. Mrs. Martin gasped and then went inside to find a blanket. All three returned to the tabernacle, where Will and Mr. Martin lifted Elijah's heavy body and placed it on the wagon. Will covered Elijah with the blanket.

"Let's pray," said Mrs. Martin. She offered an inspirational prayer of gratefulness for Elijah's life and for his family's peace and understanding. Will was surprised at her spirituality. Then he remembered the hymn he heard her playing on her organ a year earlier.

GIDEON PULLED THE wagon slowly along the dirt road to Lewes with Elijah's horse in tow. The pathway was wet but the skies had cleared, beckoning a perfect summer day. Sparrows were singing sweetly. Will could not appreciate any of this. Not only did he feel guilty about his friend's death, but he had no idea how to tell Elijah's family what happened.

After ninety minutes that seemed like an eternity, the wagon arrived in Pilottown. Will saw an elderly sharecropper preparing a field for planting with a mule drawn plow. He pulled the reins tight on Gideon. "Can you tell me where Reverend Miller's house is?"

"The preacher lives up the road a half-mile or so, but he's at the church preparing for tomorrow's service," said the old man, pointing to the small chapel around the bend. "Why you lookin' for him?"

"Thanks. I need to tell him somethin'."

Will urged Gideon ahead, and they soon arrived at the St. George African Methodist Episcopal Church. It was a small rectangular wood-frame building resembling a corn crib with dark shingles and a short steeple. A cemetery with simple headstones greeted Will as he walked up to the front door dreading what was to come.

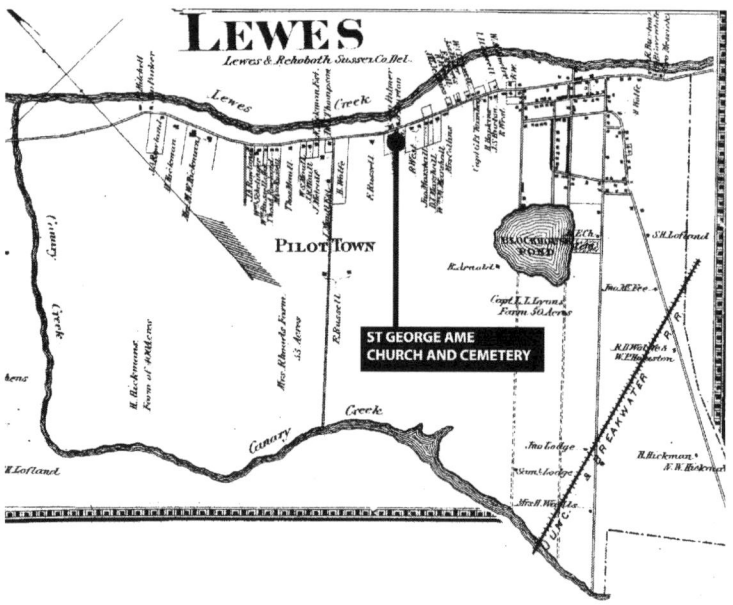

Pilottown (base map is *circa* 1868, Pomeroy and Beers Atlas, from Delaware Geological Survey website).

Will went inside and found a large Negro man in the pulpit practicing his sermon. His booming voice reverberated throughout the sanctuary, which had simple wood benches for pews. Will sat on a bench in the back and waited for the preacher to finish.

"Are you Reverend Miller?"

"Indeed I am, sir. How can I help you?"

Will sighed and said a quick prayer like he'd seen Elijah do.

"Speak up, mister. I'm busy right now," said the Reverend.

"My name is Will Thompson, and I know your son, Elijah."

"Oh yes, Mr. Thompson. Elijah speaks highly of you. Aren't you in charge of building a tabernacle in Rehoboth?"

"I am, and I have some bad news. We had a terrible thunderstorm there this mornin' and . . . ." Will choked as his throat tightened, and he couldn't get the words out.

"What is it? Is Elijah still there?"

Will's stomach was in knots. He wanted this to be a bad dream. "Reverend Miller, Elijah was struck by lightnin' and killed. I have his body in my wagon outside. I'm so sorry."

Reverend Miller's face contorted in a grimace of pain as he fell to his knees and wept. "Lord, why have you taken my son?" He wailed for the next ten minutes as Will first watched and then came over and knelt beside the preacher and cried with him. How devastated he would be to lose one of his children.

They went outside to the wagon. Rev. Miller pulled back the blanket and saw what the lightning had done to his son's body. His chin quivered and more tears flowed.

"How could you let this happen to my son? What was he doing when he was struck down?"

Will felt unprepared to deal with this and wished Rev. Todd were here to help. "He was workin' on the roof of the tabernacle. I wasn't there when it happened, but I found him on the ground right afterwards." Will failed to mention that he had asked Elijah to hurry and finish the roof.

"And where were you?"

"I'm really sorry, Reverend Miller," said Will, avoiding a direct answer. "Your son was a faithful man of God. He was like a brother to me. I wish it were me that was struck." The words seemed to come from some other place as Will had never uttered that about another man. Rev. Miller looked up at Will in surprise.

"Then I hope you'll come to his funeral and speak about him."

Will fought back more tears. "I would like that. Let me know when, and I'll be here."

"Where can we find you?" asked the preacher.

"I live in Rehoboth but will be at Bethel Church in Lewes tomorrow with my family."

Will and Rev. Miller carefully lifted Elijah's body from the wagon and carried him inside the church. They laid him on the back bench and covered him again with the blanket.

Will returned to the wagon and rode in silence back to Rehoboth. He felt numb and responsible for what had happened to Elijah. To see Rev. Miller's grieving over Elijah was almost too much for his heart to bear.

He stopped at his farm to give Elizabeth the news. He avoided explaining the details about encouraging Elijah to keep working in the impending storm and giving him the metal tools. She listened in horror. "I don't know if I can see Reverend Miller again," said Will.

"It's not your fault," Elizabeth said calmly. "You should go and speak at Elijah's funeral. I'll go with you."

Suddenly, Will felt a little better. Maybe he would go and take Elizabeth.

Chapter Nine

EPIPHANY

WHEN WILL ARRIVED back at the campground, he saw Rev. Warner's carriage. Warner and Rev. Todd were inspecting the construction of the tabernacle. "Good afternoon. It's great to see you," said Todd. "Looks like the tabernacle is coming right along."

Will got down slowly from the wagon and made eye contact with Rev. Todd. "I have some terrible news." Will explained the events of the day with a quivering voice. "Elijah's death—it's my fault. He wouldn't have been here this mornin' if I hadn't asked him to come back to help finish the tabernacle."

"Will, you did not summon that lightning bolt."

"Elijah's father wants me to speak at his funeral. I don't think I'm strong enough in my faith," said Will.

EPIPHANY

"God will give you the words and the strength. And tell Reverend Miller that his congregation is welcome to join us for services at the tabernacle next month."

"I'll do that," Will said. "There's some fried chicken in the sack on my wagon if you're hungry. I can't eat right now, but you're welcome to it."

"I'll have a bite," replied Rev. Todd. "Let's first pray for Elijah and his family, and for you." The three men gathered on the same bench where Will and Elijah had sat several hours earlier as Todd offered a long and inspirational tribute to Elijah. He asked the Holy Spirit to minister to Rev. Miller and his family. He then prayed for continued healing for Will's knee and for his faith to be made stronger in the midst of this tragedy.

The prayer gave Will some comfort, but he remained silent and unable to eat. As the preachers wolfed down the chicken, Todd thanked Will for his help with the tabernacle and asked how the construction on the other improvements was coming along.

"They're gradin' Henlopen, Rehoboth, and Surf Avenues now. And the hotel foundation is supposed to go in next week," reported Will in a soft voice. "Even Lorenzo Dow Martin is helpin' with the gradin'. I heard the surveyors are comin' soon to lay out the lots."

"That's right," said Todd, pulling a rolled-up paper from his burlap satchel. "The engineer has designed everything we need, and you can see here the draftsman has put down the grounds on paper. We hope to start building the boardwalk soon. Now

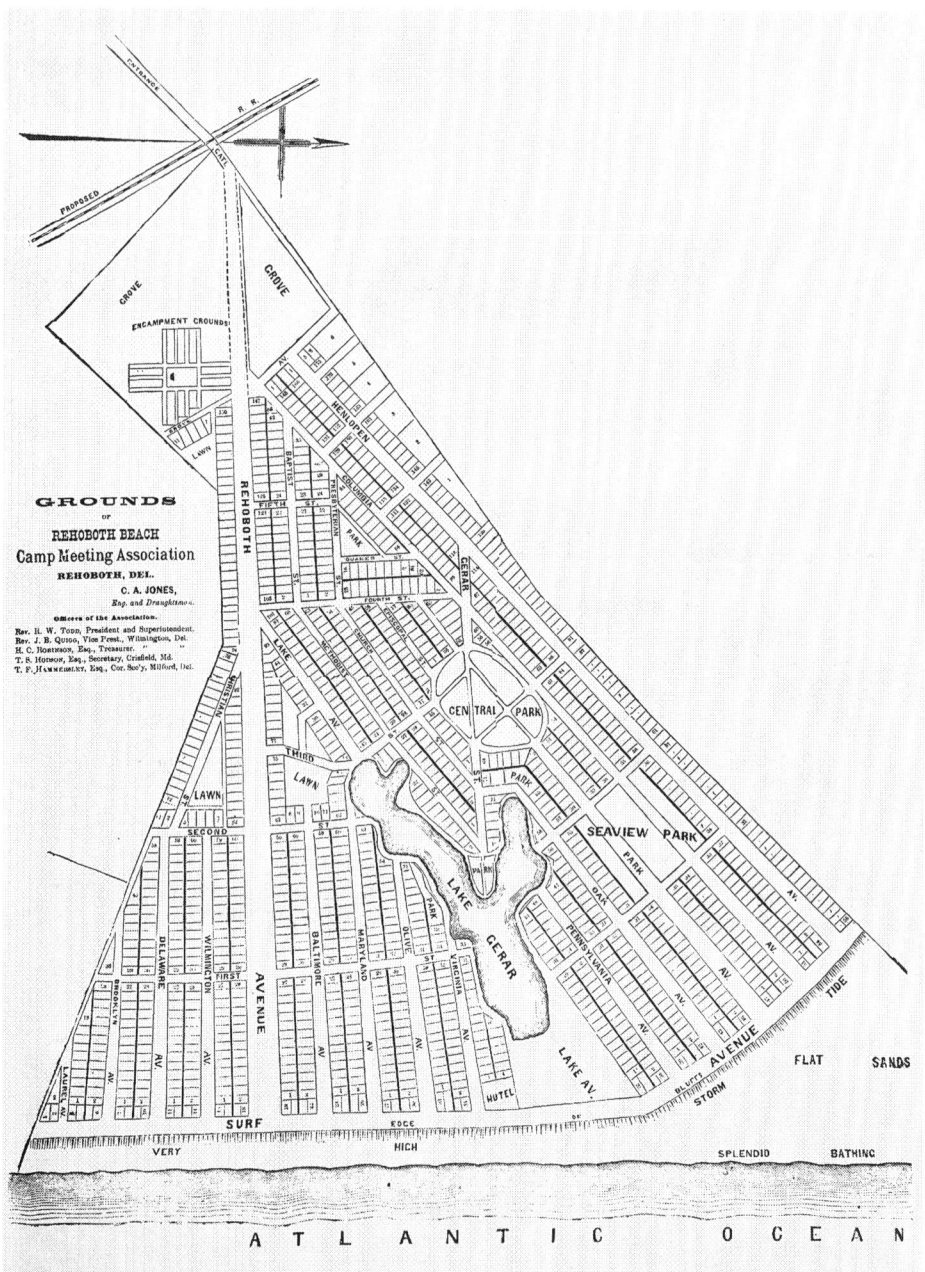

Grounds of Rehoboth Beach Camp Meeting Association (from July 1873 *Rehoboth Beacon*, courtesy of Rehoboth Beach Historical Museum).

tell me more about Mr. Martin. I've never met the man except at the other end of his shotgun last October."

"He's not so bad," offered Rev. Warner.

"Martin and his wife are still livin' in their farmhouse," Will explained. "They helped me load Elijah's body on the wagon this mornin'. How'd you get him to agree on the price for his land?"

Standing up and stroking his beard, Todd related how Rev. Warner and the lawyer from Lewes negotiated with Martin and Marsh in November after Will had obtained Martin's asking price. Pointing to the drawing, he showed Will the three other, much smaller, tracts that were purchased at the same time to make up the entire 414-acre campground.

"How'd you come up with the money to pay for all the land?"

Todd explained that he and a number of the members from St. Paul's Church in Wilmington and Bethel Church in Lewes formed a stock company to raise the necessary funds. The company was incorporated by the Delaware Legislature and named the Rehoboth Beach Camp Meeting Association of the Methodist Episcopal Church.

"This has all been approved by the church's conference, and Bishop Levi Scott and I have been appointed to run the campground this summer," said Todd. "Now let's take a walk and see how the rest of our project is progressing."

Todd took a long drink from his canteen and put the drawing back in the well-worn satchel. He slung the strap of the satchel over his shoulder and started walking at a fast clip from the oak grove toward the ocean. Will and Rev. Warner struggled to keep up as they approached the farmhouse, where Mr. and Mrs. Martin were sitting on the front porch.

"This is Reverend Todd. He's in charge of buildin' and runnin' the church's camp meetin'," Will said, gesturing to the preacher. "I hear you already know Reverend Warner from Lewes?"

"Yep. Reverend Warner and his lawyer drive a hard bargain," said Mr. Martin, winking at Will.

Todd extended his hand to Mr. Martin, who grasped it warmly. "Glad to finally meet you, reverend, when you're not trespassin' on my land," Martin said with a grin. "This is my wife Catherine, who's very religious but is Presbyterian so she won't be of no use to you."

"Mrs. Martin plays some beautiful hymns on her organ," Will offered.

"That's wonderful to hear," said Todd, making eye contact with Mrs. Martin. "I'd enjoy listening to you play. We'll need an organ and an accomplished player for our camp meeting this summer."

"Maybe you can stay for supper, and I'll play afterwards," said Mrs. Martin.

"That's very kind of you, Mrs. Martin, but I plan to have supper and spend the evening with Reverend Warner, so we need to get back to Lewes in his carriage before dark. Right now, I'd like to see how the grading of the streets is coming along."

The four men walked down Rehoboth Avenue toward the ocean. The furrows of the former corn field had been smoothed out and tamped down so it would be passable by carriages and wagons. Todd explained how the engineer had designed this boulevard to be wider as it approached the seashore so the ocean breezes would come all the way up to the oak grove.

Reaching the sandy beach, Todd climbed to the top of the dune and then fell to his knees, praising God for how quickly his dream was coming true. A flock of seagulls squawked overhead, and the men turned left and walked parallel to the ocean along Surf Avenue facing a stiff wind from the northeast.

"This salt air is the perfect antidote for my nose problem," Todd exclaimed, raising his arms in thanks. "The campers are going to enjoy strolling on a new boardwalk along here after services at the tabernacle."

As they turned left again at the newly graded Henlopen Avenue, an idea came to Will. He had been thinking of what Rev. Todd said about the need for an organist for the revival in July. Maybe Todd could convince Mrs. Martin, who seemed to know lots of hymns, to play in the tabernacle.

Will sidled up to Rev. Todd as they proceeded down the tree-lined Henlopen Avenue, which had been cut through the forested land purchased from Marsh. In a hushed voice, he suggested that the preacher accept Mrs. Martin's invitation for supper, hear her play, and then spend the night at Will's home. He was sure Elizabeth would be happy to welcome the preacher into their home for the night.

"It's a good plan," Rev. Todd said, "but I need to get to Bethel Church early tomorrow to be the guest preacher for Reverend Warner. He's counting on me being there."

"You can ride with us to church in our wagon in the morning. We'll leave early to make sure you're there in time."

Will's plan worked like a charm. When he picked up Rev. Todd in his wagon at the Martins' farmhouse later that evening, Will learned that Mrs. Martin had agreed to play her organ at the upcoming camp meeting.

"It'll sound like a real church service," Todd exclaimed. "And to top that off, the Martins have offered to let me stay in their parlor whenever I need to be here on association business."

After the children had gone to bed, Will and Elizabeth sat and talked with Rev. Todd in their parlor late into the evening. Todd told them how he had come to know the Lord at a camp meeting near his Denton, Maryland home at the age of fourteen. Before that, he admitted to being a "problem" for his parents and school masters. He was always getting switched with the hickory rod for misbehaving. "On one occasion, I stole a neighbor's pig and put it in my parents' outhouse, much to their surprise in the middle of the night."

For the first time since he found Elijah's body that morning, Will laughed out loud. Elizabeth frowned and held her forefinger to her mouth for fear the children might be awakened.

Todd explained that he'd been an abolitionist and preached against the mistreatment of slaves and freed Negroes before the war. This was not popular among many of his parishioners who kept slaves and believed that the Bible encouraged slavery. The preacher related that, during the dark days of the war in 1864, he served as a delegate from Caroline County to Maryland's

Constitutional Convention and pleaded the cause of the slave and of the Union. This resulted in the adoption of a state "Bill of Rights" in which slavery and involuntary servitude were outlawed in Maryland, except for punishment for a crime.

Listening to Rev. Todd, Will thought about how his father had cursed and whipped members of the two families of slaves who worked on his farm and in the main house cooking and washing clothes after Will's mother died. Will recalled the anguished faces of the Jackson and Smith family members who gathered with other nearby Negro families for church every Sunday. They had lived in this tiny log cabin with no heat and he barely knew their names. Only after the Negroes fled one dark night after the war did Will enlarge the cabin and equip it with a wood stove for his own family. What did the slaves say about his father as they sat in this same room?

After Lincoln freed the slaves in the South, Will and his brother were told by their father to join up with a Confederate troop in western Sussex County to fight for and preserve slavery. George didn't want to disappoint their father and had shamed Will into joining him in donning a gray uniform and training with the Confederates in Seaford. They skirmished on several occasions with a Union brigade in Georgetown and eventually joined up with some of Lee's troops marching north. While both brothers came through the end of the war unscathed, Will saw many others on both sides killed or maimed for life.

Will's father believed that Negroes were naturally lazy and not as smart as whites. Will thought about Elijah, who was energetic and had more education than either he, his father or his brother. Elijah also had a faith in God that Will longed for. How could his father have been so wrong? And how could Will have so blindly followed his father's beliefs?

The logs on the wood stove had burned to ashes, and the oil lantern giving light to the parlor was nearly empty of its fuel.

"If you don't mind, I'm going to get some rest," said Rev. Todd. "May I stretch out here on your floor?"

"You will do nothing of the kind," replied Elizabeth. "You'll sleep in our bed and Will and I will curl up with the children."

Will went to his son's bedroom and lay down next to Willie, who was fast asleep on the feather mattress Elizabeth had made. As he closed his eyes and tried to sleep, Will couldn't blot out the images of Elijah and Rev. Miller from earlier that day. What would he tell his son about Elijah? He tried to imagine asking Willie to fight in a war to justify the mistreatment of people who looked different from himself. He hugged his son, closed his eyes, and prayed himself to sleep.

Chapter Ten

THE EULOGY

THE NEXT MORNING, Will and his family sat on the front bench as Rev. Todd's booming voice filled the Bethel Church sanctuary. He was preaching the Sunday morning sermon for Rev. Warner's congregation on the Golden Rule. But Will's mind was on Elijah and his upcoming funeral.

"Jesus taught us that all of God's Old Testament law and the teachings of the prophets is summed up in 'Do unto others as you would have them do to you'," Todd exclaimed with his right hand pointed at the 150 or so assembled. "The founder of our Methodist faith, John Wesley, said it this way: 'Do all the good you can, by all the means you can, in all the ways you can, in all the places you can, at all the times you can, to all the people you can, as long as ever you can.' My fellow Christians, may this be the way in which we live today and are recognized by those we meet each day."

Todd continued preaching to the worshippers, giving examples from scripture of those who lived by the Golden Rule. Then he told the congregation about Elijah Miller's unexpected death the day before, encouraging the worshippers to live each day as though it could be their last before meeting their maker for judgment. He concluded the sermon by saying that God had used Elijah's short life to help build His kingdom on earth, including Elijah's work constructing the tabernacle in Rehoboth. Todd pointed to Will, thanked him for befriending Elijah, and invited the congregation to attend the camp meeting in July.

Will fought back tears as the communion chalice was passed down the row. He still felt responsible for Elijah's death. Why hadn't he told Elijah to stay off the rafters when they heard the thunder?

After the closing hymn, a young man approached Will from the back bench of the church that had been reserved for Negroes. "Are you Mr. Will Thompson?" he asked.

"Yes, I am. What can I do for you?"

"I'm Isaiah Miller. My father is Reverend Miller at St. George AME Church. He wanted you to know that Elijah's funeral will be tomorrow at noon at our church on Pilottown Road. He hopes you'll come and speak on behalf of my brother."

Will was stunned by this personal invitation. "Thanks for lettin' me know," Will said. "I'm glad to meet you. I'm so sorry about Elijah." Not knowing what else to say, he walked away to

THE EULOGY

rejoin his family. He didn't know if he could go and speak about Elijah. Would Elijah's family and friends blame him?

The congregation gathered for fellowship before Sunday school began. Rev. Todd came over, and Will told the preacher about Isaiah's invitation. "I don't think I can go to the funeral, let alone speak in front of Reverend Miller and his family. I won't know what to say. And even if I did, I couldn't talk without breaking down. Could you go in my stead?"

"Will, I need to get back to Wilmington on tonight's train and tend to church business. I plan to be back soon and stay in the Martins' parlor to oversee the construction. Ask the Lord to give you the strength and the words to say at Elijah's funeral. It's okay if you break down. Everyone will understand."

Elizabeth was standing nearby and overheard their conversation. She clasped Will's hand. "I'll help you practice what to say."

WILL AND ELIZABETH arrived at St. George AME Church at eleven-thirty on Monday morning. As they left Gideon and their wagon and walked toward the front door of the church, they heard the drawn-out lament of mourning doves. Then they saw a Negro man digging a grave in the church cemetery. Will stopped to gather himself.

"I don't know if I can do this, Elizabeth."

"Yes, you can. The Lord will give you strength."

They went inside the chapel and saw a large group of Negroes gathered around Rev. Miller and the open pine box holding Elijah placed at the altar. The men were dressed in black suits and the women in colorful dresses. Will and Elizabeth were the only white people in the church.

Rev. Miller came over to Will and Elizabeth and thanked them for coming. Will was surprised at the preacher's composure. He remembered how upset he was at his father's funeral and couldn't imagine what he'd be like if he were about to bury Willie.

Isaiah was talking with some other young Negro men, and Will regretted that he hadn't engaged him at Bethel on Sunday. Isaiah caught Will's eye and approached with a smile and an outstretched hand. "Mr. Thompson, I didn't think you'd be coming. Would you and your wife sit with our family?"

Will and Elizabeth approached the casket and viewed Elijah, who was wearing a bowler hat to cover his singed hair. He was dressed in a dark suit, white shirt, and string tie. His worn Bible was placed in his hands, which were scarred from the lightning strike.

Isaiah seated them on the second bench just behind Rev. Miller. After a few minutes, the wake ended and the family paid their last respects to Elijah. A large woman dressed in white, who Will assumed was Elijah's mother, kissed the face of Elijah and uttered a long, loud, high-pitched wail of grief.

The funeral service was very different from that of Will's father six years earlier. Instead of a hired preacher and his wife playing funeral dirges to a small gathering in his father's parlor, there were trumpets, drums, tambourines, and an organ playing joyful music that Will hadn't heard before. It wasn't long before he and Elizabeth were on their feet with the rest of the worshippers singing the refrains and clapping their hands.

Rev. Miller stood up and pointed his right forefinger to the cross at the front of the chapel. He turned to face the gathering and placed his right hand over his heart with eyes looking upward. He then closed his eyes in prayer. The music wound down, and the reverend began to speak about his son. He proclaimed that Elijah was a gift from God who loved his family and knew who he was and whose he was. He said it was a day to celebrate Elijah's homecoming.

"It was only fitting that my son would leave us in this way," Rev. Miller exclaimed. "His namesake, the Old Testament prophet Elijah, defeated the worshippers of the false God Baal by bringing down fire from the heavens. And he left this realm taken up to Heaven in a whirlwind."

Rev. Miller sat down, but the music didn't stop. As it continued for more than an hour, Will was amazed at how upbeat everyone seemed to be. They swayed as they sang and shouted hallelujah. It was as though they were ushering Elijah's spirit through the Pearly Gates to join other family members who passed through before.

With only the organ playing faintly now, Rev. Miller stood up again and preached for nearly an hour on what the scriptures said about death and eternal life through the resurrection of Jesus Christ. He finished quoting First Timothy and Job: "We brought nothing into this world, and it is certain we can carry nothing out. The Lord gave, and the Lord hath taken away; blessed be the Name of the Lord."

Rev. Miller invited the family and friends to come forward and speak on behalf of Elijah. Will's stomach knotted as more than a dozen men and woman extolled Elijah's virtues and pleaded with God to judge him kindly. What else could Will say about this saintly man?

Rev. Miller looked directly at Will and beckoned him to come up front by the open casket. Elizabeth squeezed his hand, and he saw the encouragement in her eyes. The knots in his stomach eased as he closed his eyes, took a deep breath, and asked for God's help. Before he knew it, Will was on his feet walking forward. He looked out at the congregation, all waiting for him to speak.

"I only knew Elijah for a short time," Will uttered softly, barely able to get the words out. "But he quickly became my friend and showed me how much he loved God by what he said and what he did. He was the first Negro man I ever got to know."

He paused. His mind blanked as he struggled to remember what else he'd planned to say. This talking in front of a crowd wasn't for him. He wanted to leave before he made a bigger fool of himself. Then what he and Elizabeth had discussed came back to him. He wasn't sure he should say anything else. He glanced over at Rev. Miller, who was nodding. He looked out at Elizabeth, who smiled and whispered, "Go ahead."

"Ever since I was a boy, I was taught and always believed that us whites were better. But Elijah turned my thinkin' upside down. He was a hard worker who knew and lived the scriptures. He helped me see we are all God's children."

As his voice cracked with emotion, Will gathered his thoughts and recalled what Rev. Todd asked him to say. "When we finish the tabernacle in Rehoboth, I hope you'll all come to our camp meetin' this summer. I know Elijah would want that, and so does Reverend Todd, who's in charge of the camp meetin' there." He turned and looked back at Elijah lying peacefully and hoped he had carried out his wishes.

The joyful music started again as those assembled sang "On Christ the Solid Rock I Stand," a hymn that Will and Elizabeth had sung many times at Bethel. Rev. Miller and the other family members said their last goodbyes to Elijah, and the preacher closed the lid of the pine box. Isaiah and three other young men came forward to carry the casket out of the chapel to the fresh grave dug in the cemetery.

The casket was lowered into the pit as several women wailed in grief. As he shoveled dirt on the lid, Rev. Miller proclaimed, "We commit this body to the ground, earth to earth, ashes to ashes, dust to dust, with sure and certain hope of the resurrection to eternal life."

Chapter Eleven

RECKONING

THE LARGE WOMAN in the white dress approached Will and Elizabeth with tears still streaming down her face. "Mr. Thompson, I'm Sarah Miller, Elijah's mother. Would you and your wife join us for a meal at our home up the road?"

Will knew he should get back to his farm to continue the spring planting, but there was something in this woman's eyes and voice that caused him to hesitate and look to Elizabeth, who quickly responded, "We would be pleased to join you, Mrs. Miller."

Will and Elizabeth sat at the Millers' wooden table with the preacher and his three children as Mrs. Miller was frying chicken on the wood stove in the kitchen. Their log home was as small as Will's had been before he enlarged their servants' quarters. The wooden chairs had spindles missing, and some of the cotton stuffing of the threadbare couch was exposed. But the Bibles, hymnals, and Christian books strewn about convinced Will that this was a place where God was honored in word and in deed.

Rev. Miller looked directly at Will. "Mr. Thompson, thank you for your kind words about Elijah and for the invitation to the tabernacle for services in July. But don't expect to see me or any folks from our church attending your camp meetings this summer."

Will's jaw dropped. "But I thought Elijah was helpin' build the tabernacle so your congregation could come and hear Reverend Todd and the other preachers."

"We were hoping Reverend Todd and the Methodist-Episcopal Conference would let us use the tabernacle when it wasn't being used by the whites."

"Well, I suppose that would be fine. But I don't understand why you wouldn't want to join with us. Reverend Todd was an abolitionist even before the war, and he's a powerful preacher."

Rev. Miller turned to Will and explained the history of the split between the AME Church and the Methodist Episcopal Church in the late 1700s, when predominantly white churches segregated black congregants for worship and prayer. His voice grew louder and the veins in his neck protruded as he told of how popular Black ordained ministers such as Richard Allen were relegated to preach in the church at 5 a.m. and weren't allowed to vote on conference matters.

"Why should the color of a man's skin dictate where and when he's allowed to worship our Lord and Savior?" asked Rev. Miller, slamming his fist down on the table and staring at Will.

ROOM ENOUGH

Will was taken aback by the preacher's action. He froze as his heart raced. Before he could answer, Mrs. Miller appeared with a steaming plate of fried chicken. Elizabeth joined her in the kitchen to bring out mashed potatoes, fresh collard greens, and corn pone.

"My goodness, what a feast," said Will, hoping that his focus on the food meant he didn't have to respond to the preacher's question right now. The women sat at the table, and Rev. Miller seemed to have calmed down with his wife in the room and food ready to eat. He said a blessing, thanking God for Will's and Elizabeth's presence at their table.

As they ate, Mrs. Miller asked Elizabeth about her children and what their home was like. Elizabeth glowed as she described her four children and complimented Will on how he had enlarged their inherited log cabin, set up a farm, and helped build the new sanctuary for Bethel.

Rev. Miller pushed his empty plate back, crossed his arms, and stared at Will. "Mr. Thompson, it sounds to me like your family had Black slaves before the War?"

Will hesitated and realized he couldn't avoid the question or lie to this man of God. "We had two families who helped farm my father's hundred acres and worked at our house after my mother passed. They left after Lincoln freed the Negroes in the South." Will was careful not to use the word "slave" and, although it wasn't the whole story, he hadn't lied to the preacher.

But Rev. Miller only stared at Will. "So how did your father and you treat your slaves?"

"Not good," Will admitted in a low voice. He stared at his plate.

"And did you fight in the war?" asked Rev. Miller.

Will continued to stare at his plate and shifted in his chair before looking up and around the table at the preacher and his family. He had tears in his eyes as he spoke. "Yes, my father made my brother and me join up with a Confederate unit over in Seaford. I didn't know any better. I'm ashamed now of what I did."

Rev. Miller glared at Will with his bushy eyebrows knitted together and explained that his eldest son, Jeremiah, was not with the family. When the family was heading north through Maryland on the Underground Railroad, Jeremiah wandered away from a "safe house" one evening to fish for the family's food in a farm pond. He was captured by Confederate bounty hunters, who got a local judge to convict him for trespassing and stealing fish, thereby making him ineligible for freedom from involuntary servitude by Lincoln's proclamation. John Hudson, a Millsboro tobacco farmer, bought him at an auction in Easton, Maryland for ten dollars, and Jeremiah was required to serve his seven-year sentence working without pay in Hudson's fields.

"That's why I accepted the St. George AME church assignment ten years ago," Rev. Miller said. "We wanted to be close to Jeremiah and welcome him home when his time came to be released. We visited him at Mr. Hudson's farm nearly every Sunday after worship. Sarah and I thought that Jeremiah, who loved the Bible, would follow in my footsteps to serve God and our brothers and sisters in Christ as a pastor. But that never happened."

"Why not?" asked Will, though he wasn't sure he wanted to know.

Rev. Miller started to respond but the words caught in his throat, and he could only whimper. Mrs. Miller had to finish the story. "Jeremiah was preaching to the other Negroes on Mr. Hudson's farm about the evils of involuntary servitude and the men who didn't want to give freedom and equality to Negroes. Six weeks before he was to be freed, Mr. Hudson told us some men in white robes and masks came to his farm in the evening, grabbed Jeremiah out of his bed, and tied him up. They took him to a tree and lynched him, saying he was preaching blasphemy against the Bible. Mr. Hudson brought his body to us. Elijah is buried next to his brother now."

Elizabeth gasped. Will felt sick to his stomach. He tried to grasp the fact that the Millers had lost two sons. No wonder Rev. Miller didn't want to worship with Rev. Todd and his white Christians. Will couldn't find any words, and there was a long silence.

Finally, he said, "I'm so sorry to hear 'bout what happened to Jeremiah. I can't imagine losin' two of your children. Elizabeth and I will pray for you and your family."

Elizabeth nodded and made eye contact with Mrs. Miller. "May God grant you peace and healing."

Will's thoughts turned to his own children, left home alone. "We need to be gettin' back home. I'll ask Reverend Todd about when your church can use the tabernacle. I'm sure he'll approve it."

Elizabeth got up and helped Sarah clear the table. They took the dishes outside to wash them using the well's hand pump. As

Will passed by them to get the wagon ready to go home, he saw Elizabeth speaking softly and hugging Sarah. He couldn't wait to get home and hug his children.

Chapter Twelve

UNFINISHED BUSINESS

TAKING HIS SEAT for worship at Bethel Church with his family, Will heard the familiar voice of Rev. Todd. He turned to see the preacher talking with Rev. Warner in the back of the sanctuary. Rev. Todd caught Will's eye and motioned for him to join them.

"Good morning," said Todd, shaking Will's hand vigorously. "How did the funeral for Elijah Miller go?"

Although it had been twelve days, Will's impression of the funeral and supper with the Millers was etched indelibly in his mind. "I learned a lot about the Miller family and how the AME church celebrates a homecomin'."

"Did you speak on behalf of Elijah?"

"I did. It was rough. I learned I ain't cut out for public speakin'.

But I invited Reverend Miller and the congregation to come to your Rehoboth camp meetin' in July. I don't think they want to attend our revivals. But Reverend Miller would like to use the tabernacle for their own camp meetings."

"I see." Rev. Todd stroked his beard. "I'll have to check and see if the conference leaders will allow that. I'm disappointed that the AME folks won't be joining us. I think I know why."

"I'll explain more later," said Will. "I'm glad to see you back in Sussex County so soon."

"Me too. The conference just assigned me to the new Rehoboth charge. I'll be here quite a bit getting ready for the camp meeting this summer. The Martins have graciously allowed me to set up an office in their parlor. Reverend Warner has offered to be my host when I stay overnight if I preach a few sermons for him." He winked at Warner. "We'll be seeing a lot of each other over the next few months," he said, turning to Will with a smile.

Will nodded. The organist began to play "I Love to Tell the Story," and Will returned to his family as the worshippers rose to sing. He pondered what Rev. Todd might have in store for him this summer. Should he offer his bedroom to the preacher so he wouldn't have to travel back and forth to Lewes? How soon would the hotel and other cottages be available for Todd to stay there?

As the congregation sang, Will's mind drifted from the church to his farm. How would he be able to help Todd and still have time to till and harvest his vegetables for market? The camp meeting was Todd's full-time job. How could a full-time farmer with four children and a wife to support find time to help?

Rev. Todd's voice boomed from the pulpit. "In Matthew chapter nine, verses thirty-seven and thirty-eight, Jesus said to his disciples, 'The harvest truly is plenteous, but the laborers are few. Pray ye therefore the Lord of the harvest, that he will send forth laborers into his harvest'."

Todd went on to say that he picked this scripture to encourage those gathered at the new Bethel sanctuary to go out into the community and harvest the unchurched to enter Bethel's doors. He explained that Jesus' ministry was performed on hillsides and on the banks of the Sea of Galilee. He noted that John Wesley, the founder of the Methodist Episcopal movement, often preached in open air venues to reach those who would not go into a church or cathedral. He finished by exhorting the laborers gathered at Bethel to invite their families, friends, and acquaintances not only to Bethel but to the camp meeting, where there would be a harvest of souls in Rehoboth this summer.

Will thought about how prepared and effective Rev. Todd was at preaching. He figured it was a gift that some men like Todd were born with but he could never master. He turned and whispered into Elizabeth's ear, "Todd could sell hay to a farmer."

"You bought his best gift, didn't you?" Elizabeth answered with a smile as the organist banged out the notes to the closing hymn.

Rev. Todd intercepted Will as he and his family were headed to Sunday school. "I'll be in the Martins' parlor tomorrow morning if you want to come by and talk about what we need to do to make this summer's camp meeting a successful harvest of souls."

"I'll be there," Will promised. "Do you need me to pick you up from Reverend Warner's?"

"That would be mighty kind of you."

THE NEXT MORNING, Will was awake before dawn and hurried to milk the cow and feed Gideon, the pigs and the chickens. There was no time to pick the early season lettuce and strawberries. He hoped Elizabeth and the children would take care of that. Will hitched Gideon to the wagon and hugged Elizabeth, who was up early to see him off. He thanked her for agreeing that Rev. Todd could stay at their home while he was in Rehoboth.

Will breathed in the crisp early morning air and said a quick prayer as he edged out of their lane and pulled the reins to direct Gideon toward Lewes. The sky was filled with puffy clouds, and the fields were starting to sprout the spring's planting of corn and wheat. He saw other farmers tilling their crops and hoped the good Lord would give them rain for a bountiful harvest.

He again wondered what Rev. Todd had in mind for him this summer. Would he need to continue checking on and helping with finishing the tabernacle, the hotel, and the boardwalk? Did Todd expect him to attend all the services? His stomach churned as he worried about trying to do all of that and tend his farm.

Todd was waiting on Rev. Warner's front porch when he arrived. The acrid smell of coal smoke filled the air as the locomotive's whistle beckoned passengers to board. Todd climbed into the wagon and sat next to Will, coughing and blowing his nose with the rumpled handkerchief he pulled from the inside pocket of his suit coat.

"You all right?" Will asked.

"It's the oak tree pollen. Gets in my nose and throat this time of year. I have trouble with my breathing most of the time but especially now. It's the little cross I have to bear. I'll be okay."

Will loosened the reins and clicked his tongue, and Gideon responded by breaking into a fast trot as they turned onto the dirt highway to Rehoboth.

"Reverend Todd, I feel bad I took your horse. You sure could use him goin' between Wilmington and here."

"Don't worry about that. I'm getting too old for that trip on horseback. The train works just fine. It gets me here in five hours. It could take five days on horseback. As a younger man, I rode the circuits and preached in dozens of small churches all over the Eastern Shore. Now my bronchitis limits what I can do."

Todd related to Will the life of the Methodist circuit rider, often preaching the same sermon to three country congregations on a Sunday and then attending prayer meetings and officiating at baptisms, funerals, and weddings on other days. He laughed heartily as he told the story of baptizing a drunk man in the Choptank River and then having to dive in to save him from drowning.

Typical Traveling Methodist-Episcopal Circuit Rider (engraving circa 1862).

They passed the tabernacle, which hadn't progressed since Elijah was struck down. Will could see the look of disappointment on Todd's face.

"I know some good carpenters from out Angola way," Will said. They could finish the tabernacle and a few tent houses in a month or so. But they ain't church goers, so you'd have to pay them."

Todd grunted and stroked his beard. "If that's what we have to do, then go ahead and hire them. Tell them we'll pay a dollar a day for ten hours of honest hard work. I'll need you to supervise them because I can trust you to make sure they're working and building it right. You okay with that?"

"I'm not sure. I have my farmin' to do, and the spring and summer are my busiest times. I was hopin' Willie could help, but he's more interested in playin' that damn piano."

Todd turned and stared at Will.

"I'm sorry, Reverend Todd. I'd like to help all I can. It's just that I have a family to feed."

"You certainly do, Will, and that's important. I don't expect you to be here all the time. And I'm going to see if the conference will approve hiring you as our superintendent so you can get paid for your time."

"I don't feel right takin' money from the church. I'll figure out a way to make time for my farmin' and gettin' the tabernacle built on time." Will paused to ponder his dilemma. Maybe it was time for Willie to take an interest in farming. And the girls and Elizabeth could probably do a little more.

"When you're here, Elizabeth and I would like for you to stay with us so you don't have to come back and forth from Lewes every day. I'll teach you how to milk my cow and slop the hogs," Will said with a smile.

"Just so you know," Rev. Todd said, "I grew up on a farm and still remember how to do the chores. That's very generous of you and Elizabeth, but I don't want to be a burden to you and your family. Besides, I'm having a cottage built on a lot I hope to purchase on Brooklyn Avenue."

"I insist you stay with us. It'll be good for the children to have a man of God in our home. Someone to look up to. And maybe you can help me learn to read the scriptures."

They arrived in front of the Martins' farmhouse. Todd climbed down from the wagon and knocked on the front door. Mrs. Martin welcomed both of them into the parlor, where a fire burned in the huge fireplace, casting a cheerful glow on the tiny room.

Will surveyed the parlor and saw a marble-top table made from the residue of some unfortunate ship sunk off the coast. The marble was placed on legs that used to be an old chestnut fence rail. An Estey organ case was perched in one corner for a wardrobe, and it was neatly papered inside with copies of the *Toledo Blade* newspaper. The walls were decorated with striking pictorial advertisements of patent medicines, including one that was promoting a "rat, roach, and bug exterminator."

"This is perfect, Mrs. Martin," exclaimed Todd, nodding with enthusiasm as he stood in front of the looking glass stroking his beard. "We can run the camp's business from here until the hotel is finished. But you must tell me," he said with a sly grin, "why you have a life-size portrait of an ugly hermit in the center of this looking glass."

Mrs. Martin peered into the mirror and cackled. "You're a lot more fun than our stiff Presbyterian minister," she allowed. "I'm going to enjoy hearing you preach to the Methodist sinners this summer."

Will and Rev. Todd left the Martins' farmhouse to inspect the street grading and the construction of the boardwalk and hotel. They returned to the Martins' parlor and sat down across from each other at the desk in two well-worn camp chairs. "The grading is coming along fine," Rev. Todd said, "but there's still a lot of building to finish before the campers arrive in July. And the stockholders are coming to pick their lots the first of next month. I hope everything is further along by then."

Todd spent the rest of the day relating to Will how the camp meeting would be organized and run. He noted that the conference had certain requirements: no dancing, card playing, or consumption of alcohol within one mile of the tabernacle, and no political campaigning or huckstering would be allowed. He explained that men called wardens would be stationed around the tabernacle grounds to enforce these rules.

"I've invited Bishop Levi Scott to preach the first service, and other attending ministers will be called upon to present the Word of God at other times," Rev. Todd explained. "We'll have three services each day along with Sunday school classes for the children and prayer circles for those adults who choose to join. Will, at one of the services I preach, I would like for you to share your 'born again' experience at Zoar two summers ago."

Will felt his mouth dry up and his heart begin to pound. "I . . . I don't think I can do that. I don't feel right talkin' to all those religious folks about myself. It makes me nervous to talk to any group of folks. And I don't know the Bible well enough if anyone asks me about it."

"I understand why you might be hesitant. But the Lord wants to use you as a channel for others who were like you two years ago. That's why God brought us together on the road to Zoar. You've changed. And He's not done with you yet."

Chapter Thirteen

ENCOURAGEMENT

ELIZABETH AND ALL four children were gathered around Rev. Todd in the Thompsons' parlor listening intently to the minister's stories. Todd was sitting in the old wooden rocking chair that Will's father had given them. Will had seen his father rage at neighbors and politicians many times while rocking in that chair. He excused himself to the kitchen to clean out and restock the wood stove in preparation for a cool evening but could hear everything being said.

"I was an ornery boy," related Todd. "My father was a serious church-goer and was quite upset the Sunday morning I let loose a frog in our little church in Denton. That frog jumped into the lap of the organist, Mrs. Shockley, who was playing 'Holy, Holy, Holy.' She screamed and nearly had a heart attack.

I learned about the persuasion of the hickory rod from my father at a young age."

"When were you saved?" asked Willie.

"I was fifteen and at a camp meeting in Chilton's Woods. Reverend Adam Wallace preached a sermon about the prodigal son and I realized I was that son who had strayed from my father's desires for me to be good and useful. I came forward and dedicated my life to Christ, a decision I've never regretted."

"How'd you know you were saved?"

Rev. Todd explained that he became a different person inside. Instead of just thinking only about himself, he started caring about others and how God wanted him to help them.

"I began to see Jesus Christ in others," he said. "Even those who were different from me."

He went on to explain that his faith grew when he studied religion at Dickinson College and joined the Philadelphia Conference of the Methodist-Episcopal Church. They sent him to be a Junior Preacher in the Dover Circuit when he was only twenty-two.

"That is where I first served with much fear and trembling," the reverend said with a smile.

"Do you think my father is saved?" Willie asked.

Todd stood up and stroked his beard. "I can't answer that. Only the Lord and your father know for sure. I can say I've seen a big change in your father's heart. For some, salvation is a process that takes some time."

Will cleared his throat to signal he was coming back to the

parlor and tried to change the subject. "Reverend Todd, what churches have you served?"

"Well, you see, the conference likes to move its ministers around every couple of years so they don't get too cozy with the local congregation. I was stationed at seven churches before my bronchial trouble took me away from preaching for nearly ten years. But the good Lord healed me enough so I could come back and get the Rehoboth camp meeting started."

Will thought about how God had prepared Todd for this new camp meeting ministry and how inept he felt to be a part of it. His stomach knotted up as he pondered getting up to tell his story in front of committed Christians who read the Bible every day. Maybe he could be a warden, but certainly not a speaker.

Elizabeth asked the twins to play a duet version of "Amazing Grace" on the piano, and Rev. Todd sang all four verses in his rich baritone.

Will recognized the tune from his painful night in Rev. Todd's tent house at Zoar. He hadn't focused on the lyrics until hearing them now.

"Reverend Todd, what is meant by that word 'grace'?" Will asked as he sat down next to the preacher.

"That's a great question. The scriptures tell us that we're saved by grace, not by our works, and that grace is a gift from God. John Wesley, the founder of our Methodist faith, said grace is God's free, undeserved favor that formed us from the dust on the ground, breathed into us a living soul, and stamped on that soul the image of God."

Will tried to wrap his mind around it. "So you mean to tell me I can't do good work here and earn my right into eternal life?"

"That's right. It's a free gift that you need to accept and then act upon it as the Holy Spirit leads. That's why you'll be given the power to stand up and tell your story at the camp meeting this summer."

Will sat dumbfounded as the twins played checkers and Willie took his turn at the piano. His entire life had revolved around working hard to provide for his family and not worrying about others. He saw something in Todd that turned that thinking upside down, and it frightened him, but also made him wonder if he could help others by speaking out at the camp meeting.

"Time for bed," Elizabeth announced to the children. Rev. Todd retired to Will's and Elizabeth's bedroom, and Elizabeth pulled a chair up next to Will.

"You accepted God's grace of salvation two summers ago at the Zoar Camp Meeting," she said. "I've seen you change into the husband and father God created you to be. Reverend Todd wants to teach you more about God's grace so you can take the next step in your faith."

"But he wants me to tell my story about Zoar," Will said, "and I don't know how to talk to folks who've been goin' to church since they was kids. I can help with overseein' stuff at the tabernacle, the boardwalk, the hotel . . . maybe I could even be a warden at the camp meetin'. But speakin' in front of crowds of people who know the Bible? That's not somethin' I'm cut out for."

"Will, I heard you speak at Elijah's funeral. It was powerful, what you said. You can do it. I'll be there for you."

Chapter Fourteen

THE LOTTERY

May 1873

STANDING IN THE nearly finished tabernacle, Rev. Todd pulled his pocket watch from his trousers and squinted to see the time. "They should be here any minute." The excitement in his voice was palpable, and Will cracked a big smile to share his enthusiasm.

The charter train had left Wilmington for Lewes at five that morning and was making several stops along the way to pick up others interested in selecting lots. Besides the Methodist laymen from St. Paul's, the group arriving soon would include a number of clergymen and businessmen, and even former Governor Saulsbury.

Although it was only ten a.m., Will could tell it was going to be a perfect day to show off the Camp Meeting Association's grounds. The sun was shining, and there was a light breeze blowing from the Atlantic. The delicate pink of the Martins' sweet-smelling peach trees that were in full bloom was in pleasant contrast with the cream-colored apple and pear blossoms on the farm next door.

Will felt proud of all that had been accomplished as he and the local builders had worked long hours to get ready for this day. The tabernacle was nearing completion, and the hotel and boardwalk showed promise of being finished in time for the July camp meeting.

Rev. Todd had spent most nights over the past month at Will's home. He taught Will how to find and read important scriptures, and he and Ruth worked to develop Will's writing skills. Will was surprised at how easy it was to learn new things once he set his mind to it.

Todd had helped him get his crops planted, allowing Will time to supervise the hired labor working to build the new town. Will had earned enough money from the conference to buy the new black suit, bowler hat, and leather dress shoes that Todd encouraged him to wear for the occasion.

Rev. Todd motioned to the west as the thundering sound of horses' hooves could be heard in the distance, followed by a fleet of several dozen carriages, coaches, and rattletrap wagons appearing on the road from Lewes. The reverend directed them to stop so the first-time visitors could climb down to inspect the tabernacle. Todd held court using his eloquent preaching style to explain how the large, open-sided structure would seat hundreds of worshippers, while the spreading oaks would protect them from the sun and rain. He then described the boarding tent and tent houses that would be arranged around the tabernacle for use by the worshippers.

Rehoboth Beach Camp Meeting Association "tent houses" with tabernacle in background and railroad tracks in foreground (*circa* 1880, courtesy of Delaware Public Archives).

Next, he led the throng for a walk down the freshly-graded Rehoboth Avenue, pointing out the partially completed hotel and the fifty-by-one-hundred-foot staked lots that would soon be selected for purchase by the attendees. They approached the ocean and climbed to the top of the fifteen-foot high sand dune. From there, Todd pointed out the finely graded Surf Avenue running parallel to the dune and a small fresh-water lake that he said would be named after the Valley of Gerar, where, according to the Book of Genesis, Rehoboth was located in Israel. Todd explained that the boardwalk, already visibly under construction, would be eight feet wide and 1,000 yards long, and would run between Surf Avenue and the dune and eventually include a pavilion at the foot of Rehoboth Avenue.

Following a country-style dinner served by the Martins at their farmhouse for seventy-five cents a head, the selection of lots by those assembled began at one p.m. Todd and the other officers of the Camp Meeting Association mounted a wagon in front of the farmhouse to announce the names of the stockholders in the order in which they were entitled according to a lottery conducted by the association the prior week. Each stockholder who paid fifty dollars to join the association had a right to select one lot.

As the crowd waited in anticipation, Rev. Todd cleared his throat and pulled a packet of papers from his worn satchel. "Folks, before I call out the names, I want to acknowledge several in our midst who have been instrumental in helping the association to acquire and build this beautiful place to honor our God."

"First, our hosts for the delicious dinner that we just enjoyed are Lorenzo Dow Martin and his wife, Kitty, who also sold us the land where we stand and where the tabernacle was built." Todd motioned to the Martins, who were resting in their chairs on the porch of the farmhouse. The crowd clapped politely.

"Second, I'd like to recognize Mr. Will Thompson, who is standing over there in the black suit and bowler hat. He introduced me to Mr. and Mrs. Martin and has been supervising all of the construction you've seen this morning. He'll be helping with the services at the tabernacle in July."

Will tipped his hat and looked shyly at the ground as those gathered cheered and gave him robust applause.

"Finally, this God-ordained project would not have been possible without the financial support of our investors who put up the money to acquire the land and make the improvements. I'd like to especially thank Mr. William Bright of Wilmington for his generous support in funding our vision." Todd motioned to the man standing beside him. Will had noticed the bearded businessman in the black suit talking with Todd as they toured the grounds.

William "Billy" Bright (from findagrave.com)

Rev. Todd proceeded to announce the order of lottery winners as each picked their lot. The Surf Avenue lots facing the ocean were the first selected as well as lots along Rehoboth Avenue near the beach. A number of those attending purchased more than one lot. Association Treasurer Henry Robinson, a lawyer from Lewes, collected fifty dollars per lot and handed out the deeds.

"Mr. Thompson, may I have a word with you?"

Will looked over his shoulder. The dapper businessman with a long white beard had his hand extended. "I'm Billy Bright from

Wilmington. I just bought Lots nine and ten on Surf Avenue and intend to build a hotel there."

"Pleased to meet you, Mr. Bright. Those are some fine lots. What can I do for you?"

"Living in Wilmington, I'll need a local man to hire carpenters and oversee the hotel's construction. You interested?"

Will looked closely at Bright and noticed an amber glass flask protruding from the inside pocket of his suit coat. "I'm goin' to be pretty busy workin' for the association and takin' care of my farm."

"I'll make it well worth your while. I have hotels in Wilmington and Dover that are very profitable." Bright pulled a ten-dollar bill from his billfold and offered it to Will. "Here's a down-payment for your services."

Will refused to take the bill. "Let me think about it. I'd need to discuss this with Reverend Todd and my wife."

"I'll be back with my architect in several weeks and will need your answer. You won't regret taking the job."

Chapter Fifteen

HESITATION

July, 1873

"SON, GET OUT here and hitch up Gideon to the wagon!" Will barked. "Gee whiz. I've got to get a move on if I'm goin' to get to the campground in time for the colored ladies to fry these chickens for dinner. There's probably a hundred folks there already."

The piano grew silent, and Willie shuffled out to help his father. Will loaded the wagon with ten bushels of corn, tomatoes, and green beans. He had killed six chickens, which Elizabeth cleaned, and was putting the wooden ice crate onto the wagon.

"Elizabeth, is there anythin' else I should be takin'?" Will asked anxiously. It was the first night of the camp meeting and Rev. Todd needed him to be a warden. The last thing Will wanted was to be running back and forth.

"Do you have your Bible, dear?"

HESITATION

Will ran inside and grabbed Elizabeth's old family Bible that she had given him after Rev. Todd and Ruth had taught him to read. Its leather cover was tattered and the thin pages had been torn and marked up by Will and those using it before him. He had been studying it every day and had learned several Psalms and Jesus' parables by heart.

"Willie, why don't you come with me tonight to help me warden and hear Bishop Scott preach?"

"Pop, I'd rather stay here and practice the new piano arrangement I'm working on."

"He can go with us tomorrow," said Elizabeth. "We'll be there as family to hear your testimony."

"I don't know about any testimony," Will quickly responded.

His stomach flipped when he thought about telling his Zoar salvation story in front of several hundred Christians. He needed to leave for the campground and decided not to push Willie's going with him even though he was growing more concerned his son was becoming such a mama's boy.

When Will arrived at the campground, he pulled Gideon and the wagon into the horse pound, where a dozen horses and carriages were already tied up. Limping, he carried the heavy vegetables and chickens to the boarding tent and was met by a colored woman wearing a white apron over her black and gray checkered dress. Her broad face broke into a wide smile.

"Why if it's not Mr. Will Thompson," she exclaimed.

"I'm sorry, ma'am, have we met before?"

"I remember you speaking at Elijah Miller's wake. I'm Anna

Dunning from St. George AME Church in Lewes. That fine young man was my nephew."

Will was speechless as he recalled the events leading up to Elijah's death that occurred in this very place. After a long silence, he uttered his condolences, placed the food on a large wooden table, and left quickly. He found a secluded area away from the tabernacle, where he sat down and began to cry uncontrollably.

"Are you all right?" came a familiar voice. It was Rev. Todd.

"I don't know if I can handle bein' here in the place where Elijah was struck down. He was in his prime. It should've been me up on those rafters. At least I should've warned him to stop when we heard the thunder."

"I understand why you might feel that way, but you aren't responsible for what happened to Elijah. He was doing the Lord's work. And look what God has accomplished through you and him with this amazing camp meeting grounds. I need you to help as a warden tonight. Can you do that? Here's your badge." Todd handed Will a large copper cross with a pin in the back.

Will stood up and wiped his eyes with his handkerchief. He fingered the cross in his pocket that Elizabeth had given him. Maybe it was time to put the chain around his neck for all to see. But he left it in his pocket and pinned the badge on his white dress shirt.

For the next hour, Will circled the campground, directing new arrivals to the horse pound, pointing out where campers could set up their tents, explaining where the boarding tent was located, and reminding folks that Bishop Scott would be preaching at seven o'clock. He heard Mrs. Martin begin to play hymns on her Estey organ. With great difficulty, he, Mr. Martin, and Rev. Todd had delivered the organ to the tabernacle yesterday.

Campers gather outside "tent houses" at Rehoboth Beach Camp Meeting Association (*circa* 1870s, courtesy of Delaware Public Archives).

There was friendly chatter as the campers recognized fellow church members and relatives from Wilmington, Philadelphia, and Baltimore who had come by train to Lewes. Will met one family that had arrived from New York by steamer to the pier in Lewes. He recognized a few local farmer families who had come in for the evening service but did not set up camp.

The tabernacle was filling up as the horn blew to signal that the evening service would begin soon. It was a magnificent wooden structure, measuring 100 feet across and 200 feet deep with sturdy oak columns and hickory beams supporting a cedar-shingled roof. The elevated preacher's platform stood at one end, and Mrs. Martin's Estey organ was prominently displayed on the platform. A cherry prayer rail was placed in front of the platform, and oak benches were organized in rows with a center aisle open for worshippers to approach the rail.

Rev. Todd opened the service with a prayer and welcomed the worshippers to the first camp session of the Rehoboth Beach Camp Meeting Association. He gave a brief description of the improvements underway, including the Surf House Hotel that had just opened, and encouraged the campers to explore the natural attributes of the area and consider buying a lot and building a cottage for next year. He also reviewed next week's schedule, which included two sermons every day and three on Sunday plus sessions for the children, all to be held in the tabernacle. Then he recognized the many persons God chose to bring this to fruition, including William "Billy" Bright, one of the original shareholders, and a local farmer named Will Thompson who he said would speak tomorrow night.

As he continued to circle the grounds, Will could hear Todd's booming voice and shivered with fear at the thought of being on stage in the tabernacle.

Before he could ponder any more worrisome thoughts, a young woman ran up to him, waving her arms and frantically asking if he had seen a twelve-year-old boy with blond hair. He joined her in the hunt for her son and found him ten minutes later admiring the horses in the pound.

"Thank you so much, Warden. I was worried sick that Matthew was lost. He likes to wander off and explore nature and be with animals. He has no father to discipline him."

"You can call me, Will. I'm glad we found him. You'll want to get a seat in the tabernacle before Bishop Scott starts preachin'. What's your name, ma'am?"

"Susanna Robinson." She smiled, and Will couldn't help but notice her sparkling eyes, pale translucent skin, rosy cheeks, and crimson lips. She saw his gaze and placed a hand on her slender waist. "I just moved to Lewes, and I'm looking for a church where I can play the organ."

As Will continued his rounds, he could hear Bishop Scott's powerful message calling for sinners to repent and come to the altar. He couldn't resist taking a break from his duties to sit in the back row and watch. As the organist played "Just as I am," dozens of men, women, and older children walked down the center aisle that Rev. Todd and he had filled with sawdust the prior day. Some were in tears while others wailed in guilt. The bishop prayed over each one at the rail, laying on hands and pronouncing them forgiven in the name of Jesus Christ.

After the service, Rev. Todd introduced Will to the bishop and the shareholders attending, including William Bright. He invited Will and Bright into his tent house adjacent to the tabernacle, but Bright declined.

"I already met Mr. Thompson," Bright said. "We have some business to discuss when he's ready. My carriage driver is taking me to the hotel in Lewes now, but I'll be back tomorrow."

Bishop Levi Scott (*circa* 1880, courtesy of *Wide Views and a Loving Heart, The Life and Ministry of Bishop Levi Scott,* Joseph F. DiPaolo, 2018).

Will joined Rev. Todd in his tent and carefully sat down on an old wicker chair with missing fibers and sharp edges. He asked Todd about Bright and whether he should consider working for him to oversee the building of his hotel.

"Mr. Bright is a very successful businessman who is well known in this state," Todd said. "He's talked about getting the railroad extended here from Lewes. That would make it easier for campers from the cities to get here for the summer revivals. And it would allow the town to develop faster."

"That also would help him fill up his hotel," Will observed. "Is he a member of your church in Wilmington?"

Todd stroked his beard and chose his words carefully. "Well, he's a member but doesn't attend much. I suspect he's been busy with his work and family. He did put up a lot of money to get the association going and to help buy the land from Mr. Martin and Mr. Marsh."

"Should I work for him? I'm not sure he can be trusted to keep Rehoboth a spiritual place."

"That's up to you and Elizabeth. Pray about it, and see where the Lord leads."

"Okay, but I don't think I can speak in the tabernacle tomorrow night," Will said with a trembling voice. "I wouldn't know what to say. Even if I did, the words might not come out right. I had trouble speakin' at Elijah's funeral. I'm just a simple farmer with no real learnin' and churchin' like those watchin' me."

"The scriptures tell us that the Holy Spirit will speak for us when we don't know what to say," said Todd. "Just be honest. Tell what happened to you. Some of the campers have similar stories of conversion. Others still need to hear and be inspired by your story to lead them to the foot of the cross. The Lord has brought you to this time and place and will not leave you alone. Pray with Elizabeth that the Holy Spirit will enable you."

Chapter Sixteen

THE PRODIGAL SON

WILL WOKE UP before first light. He slipped quietly out of bed and got dressed without waking Elizabeth. After lighting a lantern, he found his favorite rocking chair in the parlor and picked up the old Bible he'd been reading most mornings before doing his chores. He needed it more than ever this morning.

Flipping anxiously through the New Testament letters by Paul, Will looked for the passage that Rev. Todd recently discussed with him. He had underlined it and, after turning many pages, finally found verses four to six in the fourth chapter of Philippians, which he read aloud. "Be anxious for nothing; but in everything by prayer and supplication with thanksgiving let your requests be known to God. And the peace of God, which passes all understanding, shall keep your hearts and minds through Christ Jesus."

"That's a powerful scripture," said Elizabeth, startling Will. Still wearing her pink cotton nightgown, she came to his side coughing and put her hand on his shoulder.

"I need your help if I'm goin' to stand up in front of all those folks in the tabernacle tonight," Will said looking up at her.

"I'll be there for you. But just as the scripture says, so will Christ Jesus be there giving you God's peace, which is greater than you can understand right now."

Will closed his eyes and imagined 200 sets of eyes staring at him as he tried to recount his transformation at the Zoar camp meeting. What would he say? Should he tell them about the wagon pinning his leg while Willie ran to the camp? What about his hellish night of pain in Rev. Todd's camp meeting house? He'd been such a heathen mess then.

"I sure hope the words can come out and I don't sound like a fool. I need to talk to you about somethin' else. A Mr. Bright asked me to oversee the buildin' of his hotel on Surf Avenue. He'll pay me for it, but I don't think I have time to do that with the farm chores and workin' for the camp meeting association."

"We sure could use the money."

"I know, but this Mr. Bright—"

"Have you seen how dry and withered our crops are with no rain? And the association pays you next to nothin'."

It wasn't like Elizabeth, talking this way. But he knew she was right. They'd been using their small savings to buy seed and pay the vet for Gideon. If the drought didn't let up, he wouldn't have enough crops to sell at the Lewes market to make ends meet.

"And I need to see a doctor about this cough I can't get rid of," added Elizabeth. "I don't know if we can afford goin'."

These words hit Will in the pit of stomach. Providing for his family had always been his primary duty. How could Elizabeth question his ability to do this?

"Well, that settles it. I'll tell Mr. Bright that I'll work for him. And I'll see about gettin' Doc Marsh to come see you about that cough."

***

WILL SAT NEXT to Rev. Todd on the raised platform in the tabernacle that was filling up fast. He had been at the camp meeting all day working as a warden and talking with Todd about what he would say at the evening service.

Elizabeth smiled at Will from her bench in the front row. Beside her sat Ruth and the twins, wholesome and beautiful in their gingham dresses. They had their songbooks open and were singing the words of "Savior, Like a Shepherd Lead Us" as Mrs. Martin's organ welcomed the campers into the tabernacle. Elizabeth had done a good job raising their daughters. Willie seemed uninterested in being there and was watching the fireflies dart in and out of the open tabernacle.

When the organ music stopped, Rev. Todd stood up to deliver

the opening prayer. He asked for many souls to be touched and saved this evening. The campers arose and Todd robustly led them in a new hymn with a catchy refrain of "I Love to Tell the Story of Unseen Things Above, Of Jesus and His Glory, of Jesus and His Love." Then Todd began to preach a sermon on Jesus' parable about the prodigal son.

Todd read from the gospel of Luke about a father who had two sons. The younger son asked for his portion of his inheritance while the father was still alive. The father granted this request, but the son traveled to a distant land and squandered all his money. There was a famine, and the younger son had to work as a farmhand slopping pigs to survive. He was so hungry that he would have eaten the corn cobs in the pig slop, but no one gave him any. That brought him to his senses as he remembered the farmhands working for his father had three meals a day while he was starving to death. He decided to return to his father.

It dawned on Will that he was the younger son and the father was God. Many of the campers leaned forward so as not to miss any of Todd's words. The reverend closed his Bible, raised his voice an octave, and continued telling the story.

"As the prodigal son approached, his father saw him and ran out and embraced and kissed him. The son started to tell his father that he had sinned against God and against him and didn't deserve to be called his son. But the father wasn't listening. He called in the servants and told them to bring a clean set of clothes, the family ring, and sandals for the younger son. He directed the servants to kill a prize heifer and roast it for a feast. He exclaimed that his son was given up for lost and now was found!"

Todd cleared his throat and lowered his tone. "Now, the older brother had been out working in the field this whole time. When he found out his brother had come home and the father was throwing a feast, he refused to join in and stomped off in anger. The father found him and tried to explain, but the older son wouldn't listen. He said, 'Father, look how many years I've stayed here serving you, never giving you one moment of grief, but have you ever thrown a feast for me and my friends? Then this younger son of yours who has thrown away your money on wine and whores shows up, and you give him a feast!'"

Todd came down from the platform and walked down the center aisle stroking his long straggly beard. "The father said to the older son: 'You don't understand. You're with me all the time, and everything that is mine is yours. But this is a wonderful time, and we have to celebrate. This brother of yours was dead, and now he's alive! He was lost, and now he's found!'"

Todd walked back up the steps to the platform and raised his Bible in his right hand for all to see. "Folks, I believe there are some prodigals here tonight looking to be found by their Lord and Savior." Motioning to Will, Todd continued. "Now you're going to hear from Will Thompson, one such prodigal who was lost on the road to the Zoar camp meeting two summers ago."

As the campers clapped politely, Will stood up with butterflies dancing in his stomach. His mouth and throat were dry as cotton. He took a long swig of water from his canteen, gazed upward at the rafters of the tabernacle, and closed his eyes to silently ask God for strength and the right words. He looked down at Elizabeth, who was nodding as she mouthed, "You can do it."

Suddenly, an unexpected peace came over Will. He proceeded to tell the story of his unbelief in God before he took food to the Zoar campground, and about how the life-changing wagon accident crippled his leg and maimed his only horse. He explained how Rev. Todd came to his rescue, gave him a horse, and brought him salvation at the Zoar camp meeting on a night just like this. "I was that lost prodigal," he concluded, "and have now been found."

Mrs. Martin began to softly play "What a Friend We Have in Jesus." Dozens of men and women came down the sawdust trail to the altar to wait for Rev. Todd to baptize or lay hands on them.

Will realized Todd was right. The Lord gave him the gumption to do this. He stood up again and offered a prayer. "Lord, we thank you for your Word and for the salvation of all us prodigals." Just as he finished, a loud, drunken voice rang out of the dark from the back of the tabernacle.

"You're full of it, Will Thompson. You just want their God damned money. I'll bet you shit your pants up there just like you did in the war."

Will recognized the voice of his older brother George. He jumped down from the platform and ran limping to the back of the tabernacle. But no one was there.

He quickly circled the tabernacle and spotted his brother in the horse pound mounting his horse with some difficulty. Will hadn't spoken to his brother since their father's funeral six years earlier. "We need to talk."

"I got nothin' to say to a holy roller," George said. "Our father would be ashamed to hear you spoutin' off in public about Jesus."

Will approached George, who was now in the saddle and pulling on the reigns. But before he could say another word, he felt a sharp pain on the side of his face as George kicked him with his leather boot. He fell to the ground, bleeding. Just before losing unconscious, he watched George ride off.

Chapter Seventeen

COLLISION COURSE

ELIZABETH AND THE kids found Will lying on the ground at the horse pound. He was out cold with his left eye swollen shut and blood seeping from a split-open left cheek. Willie ran back to tell Rev. Todd, who immediately came from the tabernacle with two other men. They checked Will's pulse and breathing and lifted him onto the back of Will's wagon.

"We need to take Will to Doc Martin in Lewes right away," exclaimed Todd. "Elizabeth, could you go with me? These good men can take your children home and make sure they're safe."

Elizabeth climbed into the back of the wagon and cradled Will's head in her arms. They traveled slowly along the dark dirt road to Lewes, as there was barely enough moonlight to keep the horse and wagon from veering off into farm fields. The clip-clopping of Gideon's feet was drowned out by the cacophony of croaking frogs trying to attract their mates on this humid summer evening. As they passed the Presbyterian church at Midway, Will came to. Elizabeth smiled lovingly and kissed him on his forehead.

"He's awake!" she announced to Rev. Todd.

"Who did this to you?" asked Todd, looking over his shoulder.

"My brother, George. He's drunk and kicked me up-side my head."

"Why?"

"He don't believe in this religious stuff. He's never liked me anyway."

As they reached the outskirts of Lewes, it was approaching ten o'clock. Todd pulled in front of Doc Marsh's country home, which was dark. He pounded on the door, and the doctor answered in his bed clothes. Once he saw Will's condition, he helped Todd bring him into the front parlor, where a metal examining table was set up. Will groaned as they laid him down on the table, and Doc Martin lit a lantern to examine Will's injuries.

"You're going to have that shiner for a few days," observed the doctor as he injected opium into Will's arm. He began to stitch the open wound on his left cheek. "If your pain is too much," the doctor said, "take these pills—but only one every four hours. You don't want to get addicted to them. Wear this patch over your eye, and drink some of this if the pain keeps you from sleeping," the doctor advised, handing Will a whiskey bottle.

Elizabeth began to cough incessantly, and Will could hear the phlegm in her throat.

"Doc, see what's ailin' my wife," Will blurted out as he raised up on the table. "She has night sweats and seems tired all the time."

"I'll be fine," said Elizabeth. "It's just a little summer cold I picked up at church." Her trembling voice betrayed her words.

"I'm not so sure," Will said. "It could be something serious."

The doctor put his ear against Elizabeth's back and listened for several minutes. He inquired about her pale complexion, and how often she was coughing up phlegm. Then he pulled Rev. Todd aside and spoke lowly so no one else could hear.

"Mrs. Thompson," the doctor then said, "you should take some cod liver oil at bedtime and get good rest. If that cough persists for another two weeks, let me know. And just to be safe, keep your distance from Mr. Thompson and your children until the cough goes away."

"Who's going to take care of my husband?"

"He'll be able to heal on his own," advised the doctor. "And the children can help, can't they?"

As Elizabeth nodded grudgingly, Rev. Todd helped Will get on his feet. He locked Will's arm in his to lead him back to the wagon. Elizabeth followed, keeping her distance. Todd handed the doctor a silver dollar and took Will and Elizabeth home before leaving just before midnight to walk to his tent house at the campground.

THE CAMP MEETING continued with various guest preachers coming each night to share the gospel message. After two days of recuperation at home, Will returned to his job as warden. During a break in the services, he knocked on the screen door to Rev. Todd's tent house.

"Come on in. What's on your mind?"

"I've been thinkin' about what my brother did to me the other night and what I should do about it. I'm tempted to go over there and shoot his favorite racehorse."

"I understand your anger, but what would that accomplish? What would Jesus do?"

"I have no idea. I was here in the tabernacle just tryin' to help men like me learn about Jesus, and my drunk brother ruins it all and does this to me." Will pointed to his still-swollen face.

"You didn't stick around to see it, but your testimony brought more than a dozen men to accept Christ as their Lord and Savior. Do you recall what Jesus said about those who crucified him?"

"Somethin' about forgive them because they don't know what they're doin'. But this is different."

"Is it? Didn't Jesus also command us to turn the other cheek when we're struck?"

"But I can't just do nothin' and let George get away with this. I'll look like a pigeon-livered coward."

"Our natural sinful instinct, when someone wrongs us, is to seek revenge. But the apostle Paul teaches us to feed our enemy if he's hungry and to give him something to drink if he's thirsty. By doing this, Paul says you'll heap burning coals on his head."

Will laughed at the thought of dumping hot cinders on his brother's head in his sleep. "I know the scriptures say to look the other way, Reverend Todd. But George has always had it in for me, and I don't know why. It's not fair."

Todd paused as if reflecting on some unfairness in his own life and chose his words carefully. "We don't always know why someone mistreats us. You should pray for your brother and look for a chance to share the gospel with him. Then leave the rest to God."

Will shook his head as he turned to leave. "I'll have to think about that some more."

AS WILL LEFT Rev. Todd's tent house, he was met by William Bright.

"Mr. Thompson, I've been looking all over for—" He noticed Will's face. "You've been in a fight. Did you lick him?"

"It doesn't matter, Mr. Bright."

"You can call me Billy like my friends do. I'd like to know if you're willing to supervise the building of my new hotel on Surf Avenue. I'll pay you twenty dollars a week."

"That's a lot of money. How much time are you 'spectin' me spend overseein' the work?"

"That depends on what's going on at the time. Some weeks you might spend an hour a day checking on things. Other weeks, you'll need to hire carpenters and laborers and make sure they're doing their job right. Either way, you get paid. And I understand you're a farmer who needs time to take care of his crops, animals, and family."

Will thought about what Elizabeth had said about them needing the money. He decided to accept Bright's offer and shook hands with the businessman. The two of them walked down to the oceanfront lots Bright had purchased just south of Rehoboth Avenue. Bright pulled out a set of architects' drawings from his leather satchel and showed Will the plans for a magnificent four-story hotel.

Bright took a swig from a flask he'd removed from the inside pocket of his suit coat. He raved about how his hotel would become the most popular attraction in the town. Bright offered Will a drink from the flask, but after smelling the whiskey on Bright's breath he declined.

"You just wait and see, Will Thompson. The Bright Hotel will be the talk of Philadelphia, New York, and Washington once we get the railroad extended from Lewes to Rehoboth." He took another long drink from the flask.

An uneasiness came over Will. Bright's plans and Rev. Todd's vision for Rehoboth seemed to be on a collision course. And he could get caught in the middle.

Chapter Eighteen

"WIN-WIN"

THE CAMP MEETING ran smoothly for the next ten days. As word spread, more local farmers and merchants from Lewes, Millsboro, and Milton came for the daily services. The wooden-frame tent houses around the tabernacle were all rented, and arriving out-of-town visitors filled the association's three-story Surf House Hotel on the oceanfront at Virginia Avenue.

Surf House Hotel (from April 1876 *Rehoboth Beacon*, courtesy of Rehoboth Beach Museum).

Between services, the campers enjoyed walking the boardwalk and savoring the ocean breezes. A few ventured into the sharp-breaking surf. Some went fishing in the ocean for flounder and striped bass, while others tried their luck in Lake Gerar and brought back small-mouth bass to fry on their campfire for dinner.

The boarding tent at the tabernacle tried to keep up with the hungry campers who enjoyed the local produce and meats. Each day, Will brought chickens and vegetables from his farm. He enjoyed hearing the city folks remark on how his donated food satisfied their hunger.

Will's face was healing, and he was able to remove the patch and see with both eyes as he continued his duties as a warden. Rev. Todd told Will's "born again" story several times as he preached and introduced Will to the new worshippers who arrived during the second week. They sought him out to hear more, and Will began to realize how God was using his troubles to minister to others.

One of the campers who caught Will's eye was a middle-aged man lying flat on his back on a stretcher. Will had seen badly injured men in the war lying transported like this. Several men carried him into the front of the tabernacle for each service.

"What's your name, sir?" Will asked as the stretcher bearers set the stretcher down and headed for the boarding tent.

"Peter McClellan," the bedridden man said with a smile. "I've enjoyed hearing Reverend Todd tell your story."

"What's ailin' you?"

"The doc says I have prostate cancer. I have trouble taking a pee and there's a lot of pain down there. My good friends who brought me here give me morphine and help me get around. A real godsend."

This reminded Will of the story in Luke where four men brought a paraplegic on a stretcher to Jesus. The crowds were so great at the house where Jesus was healing that they could not get in. So they went up to the roof, removed some tiles, and let their friend down in the middle of everyone right in front of Jesus. Jesus was so impressed by their bold belief that he forgave their sins and healed the paralyzed man.

"Would you pray for my son?" Peter asked, jolting Will from his musings. "He has a brain tumor the docs can't fix. They say he ain't got long."

"Of course," said Will. "What's his name?"

McClellan looked hopefully at Will and smiled again. "It's Nathan. He's home with my wife, Elizabeth, who also needs prayer with what's facing her. You probably wonder how I can appear happy with all that's goin' on."

Will thought about how he would handle these troubles if he were in Peter's shoes. After all, it could have been him on a stretcher with a dying son. And this man's wife also was named Elizabeth.

"You do seem to be at peace," Will offered.

"That's because my situation is a win-win."

"How's that?"

"You see, the doc says I might live another two to three months, or the morphine could take me sooner. But either way, I'm okay with it because I've been baptized with living water. Jesus is here with me now in my heart and is also waiting to welcome me in Heaven, where I'll see him face to face."

Will looked into the man's eyes and saw his deep conviction. How could he be so content with all this trouble? Peter's friends returned from the boarding tent with tapioca pudding and began feeding him. Will saw others gather around Peter as he laughed and told stories. Suddenly, Will's troubles with his brother, his wife's health, and his concern about working for Bright seemed less important as he witnessed Peter's faith in the face of his impending death.

Yet Will felt guilty that this man's condition gave him a temporary sense of freedom about his own situation. Why was he comparing the two? He knew his own troubles hadn't gone anywhere. He would need to deal with them.

WILLIE CONTINUED TO be detached from the family. Will noticed his son becoming more and more friendly with Adam Johnson, an older boy who came from Philadelphia to the campground with his family. With Will's permission, Willie spent several nights in Adam's tent, and the two seemed inseparable.

Meanwhile, Will found himself engaging in several long conversations at the campground with Susanna Robinson. She was interesting to him and easy to talk to. He learned her husband had been a Union captain who was killed in the battle at Gettysburg. She had moved from Baltimore to Lewes to live with her spinster sister, who was helping to raise Matthew. Susanna told Will she was looking for someone to teach her son to ride and hunt.

Will thought about how lucky he was not to have been sent to fight at Gettysburg or other bloody battles in Maryland or Pennsylvania. Cousins of his from across the bay in southern Maryland were buried at Gettysburg. He wondered if they had been in the same battle as Susanna's husband, shooting at each other.

Will confided to Susanna his own concerns, which had not faded away after all. He lamented that his only son seemed to have no interest in farming. He also told her about how, a week earlier, his brother had ridiculed his testimony and kicked him in the face.

"I'm so sorry," said Susanna. "I was here when you gave your testimony. It was very powerful. You were quite courageous to stand up in front of so many people. Your brother should be ashamed." She reached out her hand to touch his arm.

Surprised by her gesture, Will drew back. He glanced into her blue eyes, and she looked at the ground. Will missed Elizabeth's touch, but knew he needed to be careful.

On the morning of the last day of the revival, Rev. Todd approached Will looking anxious.

"Mrs. Martin has come down sick and can't play the organ for our last two services. Is Elizabeth well enough to fill in?"

"I'm afraid not. She hasn't gotten out of bed for the last two days. But I met someone else who might be able to help."

Will searched the grounds for Susanna and found her teaching a children's Bible class with her son and other children. When the class ended, he approached her and asked if she would play the day's last two services.

"Perhaps," she said. "I'd need someone to keep track of Matthew. You may remember that he likes to wander off."

"No problem. I'll deputize him as an assistant warden. He can help me keep order."

Susanna smiled, and her blue eyes twinkled. "That would be wonderful. He'd like keeping company with a man like you."

AFTER THE LAST service of the camp meeting, Rev. Todd beckoned Will into his tent house. "We couldn't have done this without you," Todd said, slapping Will on the back. "I hope you'll continue working for the association to oversee completion of the boardwalk and the streets. We also need to sell more lots."

"I'd really like to," replied Will, "but I've agreed to work for Mr. Bright and I don't know how much help Elizabeth is goin' to need. The conference don't pay much for my time. And I may need to take care of my farm full-time since Willie don't seem to want to help."

"I see," Todd said with a hint of disappointment. "You need to know that I've been reassigned by the conference to the Felton charge and I'll have full-time responsibilities there. I hope to be back to preach next summer, but I won't be able to stay here and see my dream completed."

Will saw tears in Todd's eyes. "I'll see what I can do. It depends on how much of my time Mr. Bright needs. I'll let you know soon."

"I'll ask the association to supplement what the conference is doing for you," Todd said, "especially if you're willing to take a bigger role in next year's camp meeting. Thanks for finding Susanna. She's agreed to play at next year's camp meeting, since Mrs. Martin can't handle so many services."

There was much on Will's mind as Gideon pulled his wagon home. He would miss Rev. Todd's mentoring. And what did Todd mean by a bigger role for him? Had he made a mistake accepting Bright's offer? He was glad to hear Susanna would play next year, as her ability on the organ far surpassed Mrs. Martin's. He knew he would need to talk to Elizabeth about what he should do.

Chapter Nineteen

UNEXPECTED DEPARTURE

September 1873

ELIZABETH'S COUGH WAS getting worse. She had little energy and spent much of the day and night in bed. Will followed Dr. Marsh's orders and slept in his rocker in the parlor. Ruth prepared meals for the family, and the twins fed the animals and picked the late summer vegetables for market. Willie seemed less and less interested in the farm and was corresponding regularly with Adam Johnson.

Will picked up the letters to Willie at Lorenzo Dow Martin's farmhouse, which was also functioning as Rehoboth's first post office. At least two letters came each week, and Willie was responding to Adam in kind.

"Why do you and Adam have so much to say to each other?" Will asked late one afternoon when he arrived back home.

UNEXPECTED DEPARTURE

Willie was playing a new tune on the piano from the songbook Adam had sent him. The boy's answer was a shrug. But when the piece was over, he added, "Adam's going to music school in Philadelphia and hopes to be a professional trumpet player. He heard me play Mrs. Martin's organ at the camp meeting and thinks I could be famous, too."

Elizabeth had raved to Will about Willie's talent and dedication to playing, and Will was impressed with how many hymns the boy could play without reading the music. But it was time to set his son straight.

"That's hogwash, son. There ain't no need for piano playin' 'cept in church."

"That's not what Adam says. There's orchestras in Philadelphia and New York City that pay good money for piano and organ players."

"I can't understand why in the world you'd want to leave this farm that'll be yours when I'm dead and gone."

"You know farmin' ain't for me, Pop."

Will's jaw and lips tensed as he clenched his right fist. He picked up the secular song book Willie had received from Adam and threw it on the floor.

"This music is worthless. And so will you be if you keep this up."

Will rushed outside as Willie began to sob. He figured Willie's reaction was normal for a mama's boy. He needed to hear this for his own good. It would blow over.

"REVEREND TODD AIN'T stayin' in Rehoboth!" Will shouted to Elizabeth from the parlor to the bedroom that afternoon. "He's been transferred to a church on the other side of the state."

"I'm sorry to hear that," Elizabeth said as she continued to cough. "What's that mean for the association and next summer's camp meeting?"

"Hard to know. Todd wants me to do more for the association—supervisin' the build-out of the town, sellin' lots and the like. Not sure how I can do all that, work for Mr. Bright, and take care of our farm."

"Once I get over this flu, the children and I should be able to do most of the farming. And Luke seems interested in coming here to see her and help on the farm." Luke Carpenter was Ruth's new fellow. "He's strong and has a good horse."

She was choking on her words as Will came to the bedroom door. The sheet she was holding up to her mouth was covered in blood.

"Elizabeth, how long have you been coughin' up blood?"

"It started this morning. I'll be all right."

"I'm takin' you to see Doc Marsh right now."

Will ran to get Gideon hitched up to the wagon. He carried Elizabeth in his arms and laid her gently in the back of the wagon. She coughed and spit up more blood.

UNEXPECTED DEPARTURE

When they arrived at Doc Marsh's home office, it was closed and no one answered the door. Will searched frantically for someone who might know the doctor's whereabouts.

Will stopped at the Lewes Post Office on South Street. The clerk told him that Doc Marsh was out of town attending a funeral and suggested he go see Dr. Hall on Second Street.

"Hall is the best doctor in town."

Will checked on Elizabeth, who was still coughing relentlessly into a handkerchief covered with blood. He jumped in the wagon and gave Gideon the whip as they bolted down Second Street with dust flying on surprised shoppers.

"What's your name sir?" asked Dr. Hall as he opened the door that Will had been pounding on.

"Will Thompson from Rehoboth. My wife's bad off," Will cried as he carried her into Hall's front parlor. "She's weak and now coughin' up blood."

The elderly doctor examined Elizabeth, listening to her heart and lungs with a device Will hadn't seen before. "How long has this cough been going on?"

"About six weeks. I know it's probably just a bad cold, but she has no energy and looks so pale."

"Hmm. I see."

"What is it, Doc?" He lowered his voice. "Am I goin' to lose her?"

Elizabeth continued to cough.

"She appears to have tuberculosis, or what the country doctors call 'consumption.' Or TB for short. I have some medicine that can help the cough, but it's not likely she'll get a lot better anytime soon. I'll be right back."

Will groaned and his mind raced. How could he go on without Elizabeth? She was the helper God had given him. He still had four children to finish raising. Who was going to help with the farm chores? Certainly not Willie. Maybe Luke Carpenter?

Why was God putting him through all this? Then he thought of how Elizabeth had nursed him back to health after his accident on the road to Zoar. And she was the one who held him as they traveled to Lewes after his brother kicked him. He lowered his head and silently pledged he would do the same for her.

Will noticed the smell of scrapple frying in another part of the house. He wondered if Dr. Hall had a healthy wife cooking for him. The doctor returned carrying a small bottle of yellow liquid.

"This is the latest medicine for TB. I got this from my medical school in Philadelphia. When your wife starts coughing badly, put a dab of it on a handkerchief and let her breathe it in. It should help calm down the cough, but she'll need lots of bed rest. Some doctors think TB patients need to go live where the air is cleaner. I'm not so sure about that."

Dr. Hall applied some of the yellow liquid to a small cotton cloth and held it under Elizabeth's nose. Her coughing subsided, and she opened her eyes and tried to smile.

"Can me and the rest of my family catch this TB?" asked Will out of his wife's earshot.

"Not sure. To be safe, TB patients need to be quarantined.

Do you have a room where your wife can stay apart from the family for now?"

"I guess so," Will said grimacing. He thought about Elizabeth being separated from him and the rest of the family for an undetermined period of time. As a child, he had seen his mother suffer as a bedridden invalid and then die. Was this to be Elizabeth's fate?

"How long will this last, Doc?"

"We just don't know. Every case can be different. Maybe the city docs will come up with some miracle treatment."

"How much for the bottle?"

"Don't worry about that. I have three more left. I just hope it helps."

Will carried Elizabeth back to the wagon and kissed her on her forehead before beginning the long, slow ride back to Rehoboth. She smiled and promised she'd be better soon. He wasn't so sure.

THE NEXT MORNING, Will got up early to feed the animals. He noticed that Gideon wasn't in the stall where he'd left him the night before. The door was open, and his bridle and saddle were missing from their hooks.

He returned to the farmhouse to see who might've taken him

out. Ruth and the twins were still asleep, but Willie's bed was empty. He picked up a note left on Willie's feather mattress and read it with a shaking hand.

"*Gone to find my fortune and myself. Took five silver dollars from where Mother hides them. Will pay you back. Leaving Gideon at the Lewes train station. Willie.*"

Chapter Twenty

SUSANNA

June 1874

WILL HAD BEEN working at the tabernacle for the past month, helping the hired carpenters build more tent houses and construct additional benches to accommodate the throng of expected worshippers due to arrive in three weeks. The boardwalk was completed between Brooklyn Avenue to the south and Virginia Avenue to the north of Rehoboth Avenue. Will had helped the association sell more than a hundred lots since last summer, and he heard the conference was very pleased with his work.

As he cleaned out Gideon's stall early one morning, Will lamented his current circumstances. While he was being paid three dollars a week by the conference, he had neither seen nor heard anything from Mr. Bright, and the Wilmington businessman's two lots on Surf Avenue stood vacant. He wondered how the camp meeting services would survive without Rev. Todd's enthusiasm and steady hand.

Rehoboth Beach Boardwalk looking north with Surf Avenue on left (undated, *circa* 1890s, courtesy of Delaware Public Archives).

Elizabeth's condition was getting worse. She frequently couldn't get enough air and gasped to breathe. She had lost twenty-five pounds and was having trouble getting out of bed. He took her to Dr. Hall, and Doc Marsh made house visits, but nothing they gave her seemed to help. He missed his intimacy with Elizabeth and longed to be held by her again. Was he going to lose her? He said a silent prayer as he had been doing daily since their first visit to Doc Marsh last year.

Will brought in fresh straw, hay, and water for Gideon and

gave thanks for Rev. Todd's generous gift and for Luke Carpenter, the young Lewes farmer who Ruth met at Bethel Church and married in April. Luke brought his horse and farm implements and moved in with them. He and Elizabeth were very pleased with him. He was a strong and industrious man who read the Bible daily and adored Ruth. Luke was the son he had hoped Willie would become one day.

As he checked the hens for fresh eggs, his mind focused on Willie. In October, they received one short letter from Willie, but it had no return address. Willie said he was in Philadelphia attending a music school with Adam Johnson. He told them he was living with Adam's family and was very happy. Elizabeth seemed relieved, but Will still worried about what would happen to Willie. He wanted to go to Philadelphia and bring him back home, but Elizabeth objected, saying they should pray for him to follow God's leading.

Will was in regular communication with Rev. Todd through letters and conversations with Rev. Warner, the Bethel minister who saw Todd at conference meetings. Todd told Will he would attend at least one week of the Rehoboth camp meetings and had arranged for two other ministers to help with the camp meeting services. He asked Will to head up the wardens and be prepared to give his testimony.

Will wrote Todd that he spoke regularly with Susanna Robinson at Bethel, and she was excited about playing Mrs. Martin's organ at the camp meetings if it could be used. Will also told Todd about Elizabeth's failing condition and Willie's departure and asked for him to pray for both of them. Todd reminded Will that God had a plan for him and his family and to keep believing in that no matter what the circumstances.

"WE'VE MOVED MRS. Martin's organ to the tabernacle," Will said to Susanna at the end of the service at Bethel. "We should get together to figure out what you want to play at the camp meetings this summer. How about if we have a cup of coffee at the hotel down on Front Street?"

"I'd like that. Let me take Matthew home, and I'll meet you there."

Will found Ruth and Luke, who were with the twins, and together they headed to teach Sunday school. He told them he had some association business to attend to and hoped to be back in an hour. He then walked three blocks to the hotel and found the restaurant was closed because it was Sunday.

He waited nervously in the well-appointed hotel lobby wondering if anyone would see him meeting with Susanna. He fiddled with the cross in his pocket that Elizabeth had given him three years ago. He thought about leaving, but then she opened the door and approached, smiling. He noticed her bright red lips seemed larger, and she smelled of lavender perfume.

"I'm really looking forward to playing at the camp meetings," she said, making eye contact with Will. "I'll need some help with Matthew. I want him to come with me. Do you think he could help you with your warden duties?"

Will tried not to return her gaze but couldn't help himself. "It would be my pleasure, Susanna." It was the first time he had addressed her by name, and he liked the sound of it.

They discussed which hymns Susanna knew and could play. Will told her about Elizabeth's condition and how Willie had left home.

"You're a good man," she said, "and deserve better."

Will looked into her blue eyes, inhaled her pleasant odor, and felt desire for her.

"I appreciate hearin' that," he said. "I'm glad I'll be seein' more of you at the camp meetin' so we can get to know each other better."

The lobby door opened just then, and Rev. Warner came into the room bringing communion elements for the crippled hotel clerk.

"Well hello, Will," he said with a surprised look on his face as he noticed Susanna. "I thought you were in Sunday school with your family."

"Mrs. Robinson and I are preparin' for the camp meetings in Rehoboth next month. She's goin' to be our organist."

"That's nice. How's Elizabeth doing?"

"Not so well. I'm sure she'd enjoy a visit from you. I've got to git back to the church and hitch up Gideon so we can go home."

WILL FELT ASHAMED as he drove the wagon up the lane to his farmhouse. The twins giggled as Luke told them a funny story. What was he thinking, meeting Susanna alone at the hotel? His wife was ill, and here he was flirting with another woman.

As he unhitched Gideon from the wagon and turned him out, Ruth came running outside shouting. "Pappa, come quick. Mamma's not breathing!"

Will ran limping inside to find Elizabeth on her back with eyes staring to the ceiling. He put his hand over her mouth and nose and felt no breathing. He reached for her wrist and there was no pulse. He placed his ear against her heart and heard nothing. He shouted her name and she did not respond. He began to sob.

Chapter Twenty-One

GRIEF

WILL AND LUKE lifted Elizabeth's lifeless body onto the wagon. Will covered her with the sheet from their bed that was spotted with blood. He asked Luke and Ruth to stay behind and console the twins.

The slow agonizing trip to Lewes to find a doctor was eerily reminiscent of the journey Will had made with Elijah's body more than a year before. He thought back to the day he met Elizabeth at the Bethel Church bazaar. Her smile and attractive appearance first caught his eye, but it was her big heart and willingness to become a farm wife that won him over. She was always so positive and encouraging to him. He recalled vividly when she accepted his marriage proposal with a resounding "Yes, and I will love you always, Will Thompson."

He fantasized that this was just a bad dream and Elizabeth was sleeping in the back of the wagon. Maybe Doc Marsh had a drug that would bring her back. He closed his eyes and prayed for a miracle.

Will urged Gideon to speed up. Then he felt anger well up within himself. He began to cry.

"Damn it, God," he wailed, shaking his fist at the heavens. "Why'd you let this happen to her? She's a good Christian woman with so much to live for. She wanted to see all her daughters marry and give us grandchildren. How can I go on without her?"

He thought about his encounter with Susanna Robinson earlier that day. Was this God's punishment for his choice to meet her alone? He would give anything to turn back time and make another choice. And he would promise never to talk with Susanna again if God would grant a miracle and breathe life back into Elizabeth.

He arrived at Doc Marsh's home as the late afternoon sun gave way to dark clouds. The doctor examined Elizabeth and confirmed what Will feared most.

"Is there an undertaker you'd recommend?" Will muttered, barely able to get the words out.

"Well, Digger Jones is the only one here in town. He's down on Shipcarpenter Street. I can arrange for him to pick her up. Then you can go see him tomorrow about the arrangements. Elizabeth's better off now that she's not in pain."

Will directed Gideon to Rev. Warner's home and told him the

bad news. He asked Warner if he would officiate at Elizabeth's funeral.

"Of course. I've admired her faith for quite some time. She's been so important to our Bethel congregation. How are you doing, Will?"

"Not good. I don't know how I can make it without her. She helped bring me to Christ, and now He's taken her away. It's just not fair." Tears welled up in his eyes.

The preacher put his arm around Will's shoulder.

"I'm sorry, Will. Death is hard for us to understand, especially when it's a loved one. Know that God still loves you and will help heal your grief."

"Can you get word to Reverend Todd? I'd like him to attend Elizabeth's funeral."

"I'll send him a telegram in the morning. You should steer clear of Susanna Robinson. She's been seen with a lot of men in town. They say she's looking for a husband to help raise her son."

This news hit Will hard. His stomach knotted, and he vowed to Rev. Warner that he would not to fall victim to Susanna's wiles.

ELIZABETH'S FUNERAL AT Bethel Church was held the following Wednesday. Nearly one hundred parishioners attended.

Rev. Todd eulogized Elizabeth, explaining how she and Will had been so instrumental in bringing the camp meetings to Rehoboth and how he had stayed at their home.

Will sat with his children and saw how upset they were losing their mother. Ruth was comforted by Luke, but the twins were inconsolable. Will had tried to contact Willie, sending a telegram to Adam's parents, but it went unanswered.

He had arranged for the burial to be at the Bethel Cemetery on South Street. Many attending the funeral followed the undertaker's black covered wagon to the cemetery. As the pine box was lowered into the fresh grave, Rev. Warner reminded those gathered that the body returns to dust but the soul lives into eternity.

Afterwards, Rev. Todd approached Will. "Elizabeth was a wonderful woman," he said. "You were blessed to have her in your life. I'm so sorry you don't have her with you now, but she is with our Lord and Savior."

"She was my whole life. How can I go on without her?" Tears welled up in Will's already red eyes.

"It'll be hard at first. But you have four children and now Luke to help you through this. And remember that God has you in his care."

"How about the camp meetin' comin' up in two weeks? How can I be a warden at a time like this?"

"The camp meeting might be just what you need right now. And the camp meeting surely needs you, too. Reverend Quigg has been assigned to the Rehoboth charge, and he'll be at the camp all week. I plan to come over from Felton one or two nights to preach."

"You can spend the night at our home," Will offered. "You won't want to be goin' all the way back to Felton late at night."

"I might just take you up on that. My cottage on Brooklyn Avenue isn't finished yet."

Will felt a hand on his shoulder from behind. He turned to see his brother George.

"Little brother, I feel bad for you losin' your wife."

It was the first time Will had laid eyes on his brother since being ridiculed and kicked in the face at the prior summer's camp meeting. Will's first instinct was to punch George in the face. But Rev. Todd was standing next to him, and he remembered what the pastor had said about turning the other cheek.

"Thanks for comin', George. It means a lot." Before Will could say anything else, George turned and was gone.

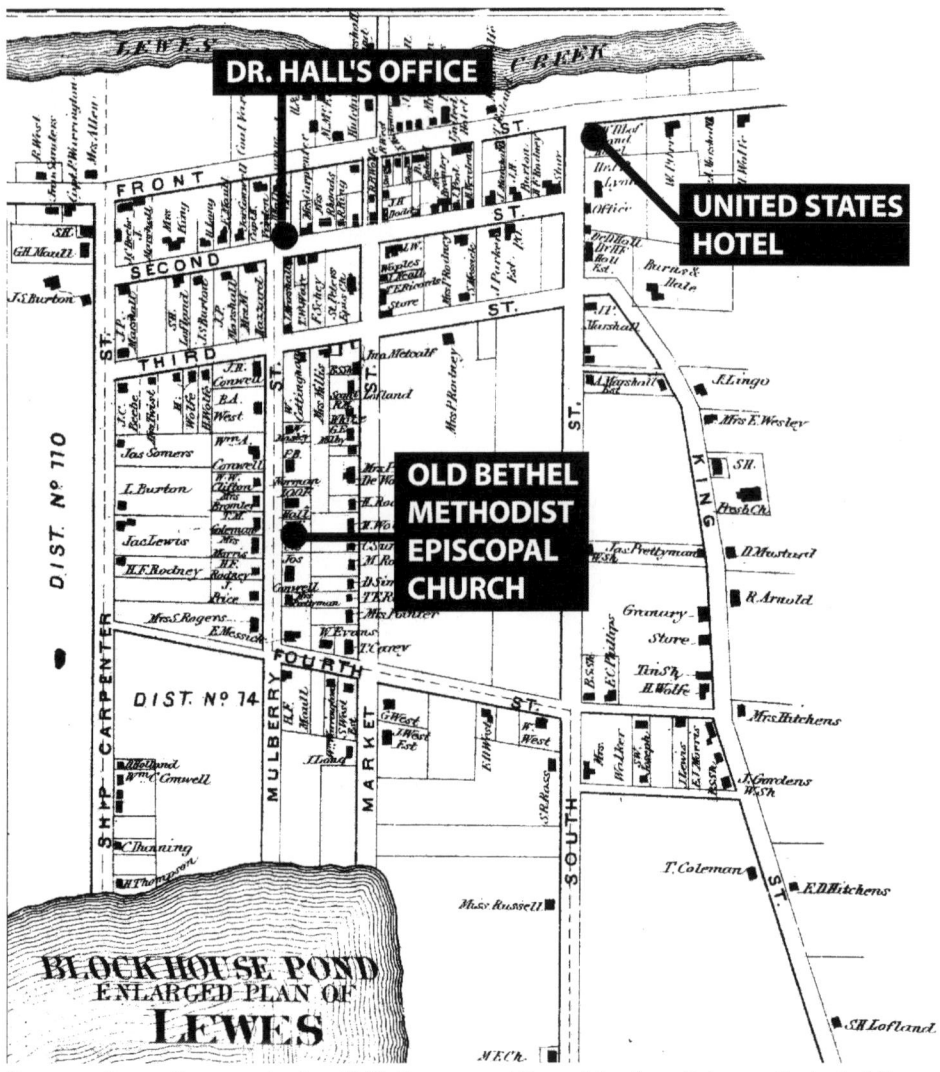

Downtown Lewes (base map is *circa* 1868, Pomeroy and Beers Atlas, from Delaware Geological Survey website).

Chapter Twenty-Two

FORGIVENESS

July 1874

"HELLO, WILL."

Recognizing the voice, Will turned around quickly to see Susanna and her son standing behind him as he stood outside the preachers' tent house waiting to see if Rev. Quigg needed his help with anything.

"Good day, Mrs. Robinson."

She was wearing red lipstick and a flowered dress with a belt that accentuated her figure.

"I'm so sorry to hear about your wife. I was traveling and missed her funeral. You must feel devastated. Is there anything I can do to help?"

"Thank you, ma'am. I'll be fine."

There was a long silence. Will continued to stare at the tent house door waiting for Rev. Quigg to finish speaking with the itinerant preacher who had just arrived.

"You seem so distant, Will. What's going on?"

"I just need to pay attention to my duties here."

"Are you still able to keep an eye on Matthew when I'm playing at the services?"

Will recalled the promise he made in the hotel two weeks before. "I guess so, but you'll need to look after him the rest of the time. Thanks for agreein' to play the organ for us this year."

"Reverend Quigg said Matthew and I can stay overnight in the tent house next to his so I don't have to take my carriage back to Lewes after the evening services. It must be the one over there." Susanna pointed to the small wooden structure to the left of Quigg's much larger tent house.

"I suppose so. Do you need help bringin' belongings from your carriage?"

"That would be wonderful. Matthew can help you. I need to talk with Reverend Quigg about the service schedules and hymns he wants me to play."

As Will and Matthew walked to the carriage lot, the thirteen-year-old boy was whistling "Amazing Grace." He stopped whistling and said, "Mr. Will, do you like to hunt?"

"I used to. Don't have time for that anymore."

"Do you have a gun?"

"Yup, I have a shotgun for huntin' birds and a rifle left over from the war." Will immediately regretted bringing up the war to Matthew.

"My Dad got killed in the war when I was a baby. What side were you on?"

Will didn't want to tell the boy that he was fighting against his father. "That's a shame Matthew. It's good the war's over."

"Do you like my mom?"

"You ask a lot of questions. She seems like a nice lady. It's good she's here to play the organ for the camp meetin'."

"She said I could be your deputy warden."

"Well, you can patrol with me while your mother is playin', but then you'll need to be with her if you're not in Sunday school."

"I'd like to patrol with you, Mr. Will."

As they carried a large trunk and several handbags back to the campground, Will noticed that Matthew was a big-boned boy with broad shoulders. He was much taller and stronger than Willie at this age.

When they reached Susanna's tent house, Will stood back while Matthew and Susanna carried the trunk and bags inside. Matthew stuck his hand out to Will and looked straight into his eyes. His square jaw and facial hair belied his age.

"Thanks a lot, Mr. Will. Let me know when I can help you patrol."

MANY MORE WORSHIPPERS were coming for this year's camp meeting. Rev. Quigg said the word was out about Rehoboth and its healthy seaside features. The tabernacle was nearly full for every service, and the evening services were standing room only as the local farm families came to hear the preaching. Rev. Todd arrived mid-week and spent two nights at Will's home, sleeping in the same bed where Will found Elizabeth's lifeless body two weeks earlier.

Rev. J.B. Quigg (undated, courtesy of Barratt's Chapel & Museum).

The second night after services, Will and Todd sat on Will's front porch after the rest of the family had turned in. Will brought out the bottle of whiskey that Doc Marsh had given him and offered the preacher a drink.

"I don't partake in red-eye, Will. But you go ahead."

Will poured himself a good measure into a tin cup and began sipping the alcohol. It was a clear night and the stars and nearly full moon lit up the sky and lane in front of them. Fireflies danced in the distance, and the male cicadas buzzed their high-pitched mating call.

"I remember sittin' here with Elizabeth many a night," said Will, his voice cracking. "I never thought I'd be without her." He buried his head in his hands and began to sob.

Rev. Todd put his arm around Will, squeezing his shoulder with his hand. There was a long silence.

"I think God took her to punish me."

"Why do you say that?"

Will explained his private meeting with Susanna at the hotel as tears flowed down his cheeks.

"Elizabeth had been sick for so long, and I was attracted by Susanna's looks. I didn't ever touch her, but I wanted to. I feel so bad about that."

Rev. Todd stroked his beard pensively and cleared his throat.

"You aren't the first Christian man to be tempted. I had to fight my own urges as well, especially as a younger man. Recall in the eighth chapter of John that Jesus forgave the adulterous woman. It wasn't your fault God took Elizabeth. And Jesus can forgive you for your sinful thoughts."

"But then why did God take her from me and her family?"

"We can't know all of God's plans. That's the great mystery of life. But all will be revealed in God's perfect timing. You must trust in that."

"I don't know what to make of Susanna Robinson. I'm goin' to be seein' her every day at the camp meetin' and helpin' out with her son. Reverend Warner told me to be careful. They say she's been with a lot of men and is lookin' for a father for her son."

"Give it some time. Not everything you hear is true. Gossip is a sin that traps many. Susanna will be helping a lot of folks find the Lord through her music. Get to know her before you make any judgments."

Will finished the cup of whiskey. He thought about what he had just heard and started to feel better. Was it the whiskey or Rev. Todd that calmed his guilt? He wasn't sure. As he turned in for the night, he slipped to his knees and prayed for forgiveness.

Chapter Twenty-Three

THE RESCUE

AS THE REHOBOTH Camp Meeting entered its second week, it continued to draw hundreds of worshippers to each service. All of the tent houses surrounding the tabernacle were rented, and the association's Surf House was full. Morning services were held on the beach, where the rising sun over the water and the salt air engendered heartfelt testimonies among the faithful.

The fiery preaching and Susanna's stirring hymns brought dozens down the sawdust trail to the altar. Matthew happily followed Will as he policed the tabernacle grounds while Susanna played. Will couldn't help but notice Susanna's skill and fervor in playing Mrs. Martin's organ.

Bishop Scott preached a powerful sermon on the Prodigal Son on the last night after Will delivered his testimony. With tears in his eyes, Will explained how Elizabeth had been taken from him and his family. He closed by saying that he knew she was no longer suffering and was rejoicing with her Lord and Savior Jesus Christ.

Bishop Levi Scott (*circa* 1880, courtesy of *Wide Views and a Loving Heart, The Life and Ministry of Bishop Levi Scott*, Joseph F. DiPaolo, 2018).

As he made his rounds outside the tabernacle, Will glanced at the long line of worshippers waiting to be baptized by Bishop Scott. He couldn't believe his eyes. There was his brother George kneeling at the altar as the bishop anointed his head with water and said a prayer into his ear.

After the service, Will left Matthew by the preachers' tent and tracked George down at the horse pound as thunder rumbled in the distance.

"I'm surprised to see you here," Will said. "What's goin' on?"

"I need to change my life," George said. "The bottle's goin' to kill me."

"Why don't you come to church in Lewes with me and my family."

"I don't know about that," George replied, mounting his horse. "I can't handle too much religion."

"How 'bout comin' to dinner one Sunday? My daughter Ruth can fix some good chicken and dumplings. You can bring your wife and kids."

"My wife run off, and my son won't speak to me. It's just me and my horses."

"Really? Maybe they'll come back if you give up drinkin'."

"We'll see. I'll think about comin' to dinner. How's your son?"

Will hesitated. He wasn't sure how much to say about Willie. The thunder was coming closer. "He's goin' to school up in Philly."

"I didn't see him at Elizabeth's funeral."

Thunder rumbled overhead, and Will paused to looked up at the sky. "Yeah, he couldn't make it in time."

George waited for his brother to say more, but Will bit his lip as lightning flashed in the distance.

"These God damn boys have minds of their own," George said as he pulled on the reins and gave his horse a kick. "I've got to get back to the farm and put up my horses before this storm hits."

WILL HOBBLED BACK to the preachers' tent. He knocked on the screen door of Susanna's tent house. There was no response. Matthew was nowhere in sight. Hundreds of worshippers were leaving the tabernacle as Susanna played the last hymn.

Circling the campground, Will inspected every tent house in search of the boy. Finally, he approached Susanna, who was putting her sheaf of music in a brown satchel.

"I don't know where Matthew is," Will said, perspiration covering his brow.

"I thought he was with you."

"He was, but I left him by the preachers' tent while I went to talk with my brother at the horse pound. Did you see him?"

"No. I'm worried he may have gone down to the ocean. He's been watching the waves with awe as others waded in, but he can't swim." Tears began to well up in her eyes. "He told me this morning he wanted to see what it felt like to ride a wave."

The storm was getting closer. Raindrops began to fall.

"I'll go look for him."

Will limped as fast as he could back to the horse pound. He jumped on Gideon and galloped down Rehoboth Avenue to the beach. He scanned the rough surf as the wind picked up and lightning lit up the sky. Rain was now coming down in buckets.

The lightning illuminated a head bobbing just beyond where the

THE RESCUE

waves were breaking. It was Matthew struggling to keep himself afloat. Will could faintly hear his voice screaming for help as the surf crashed around him and the thunder roared overhead.

Will recalled his own limitations in deep water and looked around for someone else to help him. But no one was there, so he urged Gideon to charge into the surf. The faithful steed responded by breeching the breaking waves and heading for Matthew as the storm swirled around them. When they got within five feet of the boy, Will tried to throw him one end of the rein while holding firmly to the other end. On the third try, the rein landed next to the boy.

"Grab it and I'll pull you to shore!" Will yelled.

Lunging toward shore, Matthew was able to clutch the rein in his right hand. Will pulled the boy toward him and then locked his arm around his shoulder and armpit. He used the other rein to turn Gideon toward the shoreline. Together they pulled Matthew out of the deep water and beyond where the waves were breaking. Will jumped down into the shallow water and dragged Matthew up to the sandy beach.

Will laid Matthew on his back, put his hands on top of each other and pressed up and down on his chest as he had seen his father do once. Seawater flowed from the boy's mouth, and his glazed eyes opened wide as he shivered. After a few minutes, Matthew regained full consciousness.

"I'm so sorry, Mr. Will. I thought I could teach myself to swim. I was doin' okay until the storm came in and the waves got too big."

Will helped Matthew to his feet and gave him a hug.

"Let's get you back to the campground. Your mother doesn't know where you are and is worried sick. Thank God you held on until Gideon and I got here."

Will lifted the boy into Gideon's saddle in front of him and held him with one arm. They rode slowly back to the campground as the skies cleared and a full moon rose over the horizon.

"Praise God you're safe," exclaimed Susanna, throwing her arms around Matthew as Will brought him into her tent house. "Where were you?"

"Getting a swimming lesson from Mr. Will," the boy answered with a smile.

Chapter Twenty-Four

ORDINATION

January 1875

"PLEASE READ THE Gospel of John and let's discuss it next week," said Rev. Pegg as Will gathered up his papers and Bible to leave the Bethel Church in Lewes.

"Yes, sir," Will said with a grin, as he left Pegg's office and went to see if Susanna's Sunday school class had finished.

For the past four months, as recommended by Rev. Todd, Will had been studying under Bethel's new pastor in hopes of becoming a licensed local preacher in the Methodist-Episcopal Church. He knew this wouldn't result in ordination as a full-fledged minister, but it would allow him to preach and perform weddings and funerals.

For Will, the course of study had been an intense immersion into not only the Bible, but also the teachings of John Wesley and the rules and procedures of the Wilmington Conference of the Methodist-Episcopal Church.

If he stayed on schedule, Will could complete the coursework by the end of February and be put on trial for admission at the annual meeting of the Wilmington Conference to be held in Smyrna in March. Bethel already had one local preacher, but he was in his late seventies and suffering with dementia. Will saw this as an opportunity not only to help the Bethel congregation but play a larger role in the camp meetings at Rehoboth.

Susanna had encouraged Will to pursue his new vocation. After he saved Matthew in the ocean, he had supper with them at Susanna's home after Sunday services on three occasions. Susanna's sister had married and moved to Milton with her shipbuilder husband and allowed Susanna and Matthew to stay in her Lewes home.

Will engaged in deep conversations with Susanna about her upbringing, her time in Lewes, and her expectations for the future. He discovered that she was a wholesome woman with a strong spiritual foundation. Matthew regularly talked with Will about farming, hunting, and the Bible. While he enjoyed his time with Susanna and Matthew, he never spent the night with them.

"How was your class with Reverend Pegg today?" asked Susanna as she closed the door to the Sunday school classroom, where she had been teaching Matthew and other children his age.

"It went well. We covered the Gospel of Luke and some of the conference's restrictions on drinkin' and sellin' alcohol, dancin' and card-playin'."

"What do you think about those rules?"

"I suppose it makes sense. The bottle has ruined many a man. But I wonder if bein' against dancin' and card-playin' is keepin' some folks from comin' to church and bein' judged for that. What do you think?"

"I like to dance. It makes me feel like I'm in Heaven. But I don't do it publicly."

"I never learned to dance, but I used to drink a lot and play poker for money when I was in the army. Elizabeth helped me see the evil in that and didn't want our children to follow in my footsteps. So I quit both."

"You must have really loved her."

Will nodded. "She was a good wife. I miss her every day."

Will turned away so Susanna wouldn't see his lip quiver and a tear start to form. He reached into his suit jacket pocket to pull out a handkerchief and blow his nose.

"She was lucky to have you as a faithful husband and father to your children."

"Let's find Matthew and get some supper at the hotel," Will said as he returned his handkerchief to his pocket.

"I don't think the hotel's restaurant will be open on Sunday. I have some beef stew that's been simmering all night in hopes that you'd join Matthew and me this afternoon."

"That's right. I forgot they'd be closed today." Will suddenly felt sick to his stomach as he recalled meeting Susanna after church at the hotel nearly two years ago on the day Elizabeth died. "I better get back to the farm and start readin' John."

As Will went to the church paddock to find Gideon, he saw his brother leaving the church. A stiff cold wind was blowing in from the bay, and Will pulled up the collar of his coat and reached into his saddlebag for his rawhide gloves.

"Well, hello, little brother," said George, slapping Will on the back. "I'm learnin' a lot from Reverend Pegg and the adult Sunday school here at Bethel. They seem to really appreciate my tithin'. What've you been up to?"

Will hesitated, recognizing the hubris in his brother's voice. He knew that he'd never be in a position to put as much money in the collection basket as George. "How 'bout comin' over for some dinner this evenin'?"

"Naw, I got letters I need to respond to. Did you see where I offered to lease my farm out for this summer?"

"No, I didn't."

"Yup. All three hundred acres, farmhouse, barn, stables, and ice house located perfectly between the camp meetin' grounds and Lake Newbold. It should fetch a pretty penny from some of those City folks comin' to the ocean."

George mounted his sleek Arabian and turned to head out of the paddock as snow began to fall.

"Where will you stay this summer?" asked Will.

"Reverend Pegg says I can have a room at the Surf House all summer at no cost so long as I help out at the camp meetin'."

"What does he want you to do?"

"Not sure yet. Maybe some kinda warden."

Riding home on Gideon, Will didn't know whether to be happy

or not about the news from George. It was good that his brother was becoming more involved with the church, but he wasn't sure he could trust his brother's behavior at the camp meeting, especially to be a warden. He reached up and touched the scar from George's boot that was still visible on his left cheek. He wondered how much his brother had really changed.

"I'M SO PROUD of you," Rev. Todd exclaimed, throwing his arm around Will. Rev. Quigg, the Presiding Elder of the Wilmington Conference, stood with them and extended his hand to Will, who had just been ordained as a deacon and local preacher by the conference at its annual March meeting in Smyrna.

"You'll be a big help to Reverend Pegg at Bethel and at the camp meeting in Rehoboth," said Quigg. "The prospects for this summer's camp meeting are good, but we have a lot of work to do to get ready for the camp in July. I hope you'll help with some of the preaching, including sharing your testimony as you did last summer."

Will felt a sense of relief after learning he had passed the grueling trial of the examining committee a day earlier. But he also worried that he might not live up to the expectations of Todd and Quigg. On the train ride back to Lewes with Rev. Pegg, he learned what Pegg had in mind for him at Bethel, and his anxiety increased.

"I expect my local preacher to handle the Sunday service once a month and preach the sermon," Pegg explained.

"I'll try to do my best, but I still have a farm to take care of and a family to feed," said Will, his voice going up an octave as they passed east of Georgetown and he saw farmers already plowing their fields for spring planting.

Pegg turned and looked Will squarely in his eyes. "God will never ask you to do more than you can handle. You'll need to be in prayer every morning asking what He would have you do."

Will felt embarrassed for his lack of faith and decided to change the subject. "Thanks for invitin' my brother George to join the congregation. He seems to be transformed."

"I think you're right about that. I see him being a big help at the camp meeting this summer."

"What will he be doing?"

"Reverend Quigg and I want him to lodge at the Surf House and keep an eye on what's happening there. We need to make sure there's no alcohol, dancing, card-playing, or other amusements at the association's hotel. We also may ask him to help you with the warden duties at the camp meeting grounds, since we expect a large turnout this year. What do you think of him being a warden?"

The train slowed and blew its whistle as it entered Lewes and crossed South Street before stopping at the station on King's Highway.

"I suppose I'll need to pray about that."

Chapter Twenty-Five

SIBLING RIVALRY

July 1875

WILL MET WITH Rev. Pegg after the Sunday service at Bethel to prepare for the camp meeting set to begin in Rehoboth in two weeks. He sat in a wooden straight-back chair in the preacher's closet-sized office that was filled with piles of religious books, Bibles, Methodist Conference minutes, and sermon notes. Since he was being paid by the association to oversee the construction and repair of association assets, Will figured it was a good time to report on the work that had been accomplished in Rehoboth since last summer's meeting.

"The tabernacle and surroundin' buildings have been fenced in to keep runaway horses from disruptin' the services," Will explained. "A large new boardin' tent and a dozen new frame tent houses surroundin' the tabernacle are finished and now available for rent. I understand they go for eight to twelve dollars a week dependin' on location and size."

Will advised Pegg that repairs had been made to the Surf House, and that an oval-shaped pavilion twenty-five feet across had been constructed on the boardwalk at the foot of Rehoboth Avenue for religious and other purposes.

Pegg removed several newspaper clippings from his desk drawer and pulled out wire-rimmed glasses from his waistcoat pocket to read the fine print. He reported that the association had spent more than $100,000 on improvements in Rehoboth, and over half of the 1400 lots had been sold for $100-$500 each, depending on location. He described with interest that the Old Dominion Steamship Company had bought the Junction and Breakwater Railroad Company and planned to extend the rail line from Lewes to Rehoboth.

"Old Dominion ran streamers three days a week from Philadelphia to Lewes during the camp last year," said Pegg. "Looks like they want to expand their empire in southern Delaware."

Will removed his bowler hat and fanned himself. The summer heat and humidity had arrived in Lewes. "What are you and Reverend Quigg lookin' for me to do at this year's camp meetin'?" he asked.

"I'd like for you to take charge of one of the services during each week of the camp. That would include preaching the sermon, leading prayer and singing, and baptizing any who are converted and come to the altar." Rev. Pegg said. "How do you feel about that?"

"What should I preach on? I've never done anythin' more than tell my story."

"That's up to you. You can give your testimony, but you'll need to tie it to some scripture."

"Will you help me with the scripture part?"

"I will indeed," said Pegg as he stood up and put the clippings back in his desk drawer. "Write something up, and I'll take a look at it. Then you can preach it to me first."

"What about my warden duties?"

"Reverend Quigg and I've decided to let your brother do that. We'd like you to be available to help out as needed with the services, handle some Sunday school classes, and pray with the families tenting around the tabernacle. We also plan to have some prayer and testimony gatherings on the beach in front of the Surf House where you could help."

"Hmm. I hope George can handle that. You know what I mean?"

"Keep an eye on him, and let us know if you see any problems. Please let him know we want him to be the warden and fill him in on what he's to do."

Will nodded. As he left Pegg's office, an uneasy feeling came over him thinking about his new responsibilities and having to rub elbows with George for two weeks.

"REVEREND PEGG WANTS me to take on a different role at the camp meetin' this year," Will said to Susanna as he put wood in the kitchen stove at her home on South Street.

They had just returned from church a week before the camp meeting was to begin. She was wearing a pretty periwinkle blue and cream flowered dress. Will noticed her lavender perfume and the long wavy blonde hair that flowed over her shoulders.

"How's that?" she asked.

"I'll need to be preachin' and runnin' around the campground and downtown. They want my brother to be the new warden."

"So you won't be able to be with Matthew?" she asked in a low voice so Matthew, who was playing croquet outside, wouldn't hear. "He really looks up to you. I don't want him hanging around your brother based on what you've told me."

"I like Matthew and want to help with him. I just don't know how it'll work out right now."

"He's starting to feel his oats," Susanna said, looking directly at Will. "I can't be playing at the services if he's not being watched."

Will recalled Matthew's near drowning the prior summer. He also knew they needed Susanna playing the organ at the services because it stirred folks up to come to the altar. "I'll talk with Pegg and see what we can do," said Will.

She reached for Will's hand and gave him a peck on his scarred cheek. "I'd really appreciate that. I hope you'll stay for dinner and spend some time with Matthew and me. We're having chicken and dumplings."

"That's my favorite," Will said as he removed his Sunday suit coat. "I guess my family's gettin' used to me bein' here on Sunday afternoons, and I really enjoy your company."

"YOU'LL NEED TO keep a close watch on what goes on at the campground, especially at the evenin' services," Will told his brother as they met in the parlor of the Surf House. "Some of the local men may come in two sheets in the wind. We can't have them disruptin' the preachin'."

"I know a little 'bout that," George said with a chuckle as he puffed on what remained of his foul-smelling cigar.

"And you'll need to seize any playin' cards and bottles of lush you come across. There's some folks that come to camp lookin' for somethin' different than a religious experience."

George pushed the cigar stub into an ash tray and looked squarely at Will. "I know what I'm doin', little brother. You don't need to lecture me, or I'll kick the shit out of you again."

Will recoiled. Same old George, he thought.

"I hear tell you're sweet on the organist at church," George clucked. "Will she be playin' at the camp?"

Will felt his face flush. "She's a fine Christian lady."

"She's very fetchin'. I'd like to get to know her."

Chapter Twenty-Six

APPEARANCES

BISHOP SCOTT'S POWERFUL sermon on Saturday night entitled "Come to the Throne with Boldness" drew a large gathering. After the bishop's entreaty, more than twenty repentant worshippers came forward to the altar seeking forgiveness.

Will attended all of the services and sat with Matthew while Susanna rallied the worshippers with her energetic and inspiring renditions of well-known hymns and newer songs such as "Blessed Assurance, Jesus is Mine" with its catchy refrain, "This is my story, this is my song, praising my Savior all the day long."

After the service, Will asked Susanna about the new tune.

"That was written by Fanny Crosby," she explained, "who was blind from infancy but penned thousands of hymns and gospel songs. I love her works because they're so easy to understand and sing. They're perfect for revivals like this camp meeting."

"That one sure brought the sinners to their knees. We're so lucky to have you playin' for us."

Rev. Pegg delivered the Sunday evening sermon. "Blessed be the Lord God of Israel for He hath visited and redeemed his people." Again, many came forward to give their lives to Christ.

TWO DAYS LATER, Will followed these polished preachers to the pulpit at an afternoon service, relating his salvation story to the Prodigal Son parable from Luke Chapter Fifteen. Rev. Quigg commended him on his preaching and handling of the service, though Will noticed the tabernacle was only half full.

Afterwards, Will, Susanna, and Matthew walked down Rehoboth Avenue to the association's Surf House to attend a prayer meeting on the beach. Will noticed that the hotel was full, and he saw a lot of folks in bathing suits and casual wear relaxing on the beach and porch. These were people who hadn't attended the service. There were families frolicking in the surf, where a staked rope provided assurance for poor swimmers. Will wondered why these Christians chose not to come to his service.

The prayer meeting on the sand dune in front the hotel also

was sparsely attended. As they headed from the beach across the boardwalk after the meeting, George was waiting for them, puffing on a cigar.

"Hello, little brother. Who's this fine-lookin' lady you're escortin'?"

Will paused, remembering his brother's previous comments about Susanna. He pondered how much he should tell him.

"This is Miss Robinson, our accomplished organist from Bethel Church who is playin' at the camp meetin'. Susanna, this is my brother, George."

"Pleased to meet ya. I'm familiar with Miss Robinson's talent on the organ at Bethel. It's the sweetest music I've heard since our mama used to play the piano. And who's this broad-shouldered young man?" asked George, motioning to Matthew.

"This is Miss Robinson's son, Matthew," Will said. "He was my deputy warden last year." As soon as the words left his lips, Will regretted saying them.

"Son, you probably noticed I'm the new warden at the tabernacle," George said. "You're welcome to be my deputy."

"Thank you, but Matthew's going to be too busy helping your brother," piped in Susanna.

"Miss Robinson, ain't you stayin' in the tent house next to the preachers' tent?" asked George.

"Yes, that's right."

"I'll be keeping a close eye on your tent, since you're a single woman."

"Thank you, Mr. Thompson, but I'll be just fine."

George took a long draw on his cigar, winked at Will, and retreated into the Surf House as the dinner bell rang.

AFTER THIS ENCOUNTER with his brother, Will stayed close to Susanna and Matthew. He spent a lot of time in their tent house, particularly in the evenings, at the request of Susanna. However, he continued to go home late each night after he was sure George had returned to the Surf House. He would check on his farm and family and then return early in the next morning. He showed Matthew how to shoot his rifle and left it with him when he departed for the evening, advising the boy to protect his mother from intruders.

During this time, Will and Susanna had become much closer. One evening after the service, Matthew fell asleep early in the tent house. Susanna told Will how proud she was of him for becoming a local preacher and playing such a significant role in the camp meeting, including leading a service. She admitted being frightened by George and said she was glad Will was looking after her.

"I'm happy to help you any way I can," Will said. "I feel like you understand me and care about me."

"I do. And Matthew has grown to love you like a father."

Will moved from his chair to the cot, where Susanna sat with her elbows on her knees and hands resting on her cheeks. Her face glowed in the flickering light of the oil lamp, a smile welcoming his gaze. The lace bodice of her tight-fitting dress led his eyes to her soft neck, and below, the swell between her breasts ignited his imagination. She reached out her hand and placed it gently on Will's forearm. Will turned and engulfed her with his arms, their lips meeting for the first time. Her passionate response was more than he hoped for as he kissed her deeply on the lips. When Matthew stirred, Will retreated to his chair. Susanna smiled at him.

THE CAMP MEETING Association stockholders met on the next to last day of the camp in the preachers' lodge. Rev. Quigg was in attendance as well as Billy Bright and a number of other directors who were not preachers and carried proxies from other more secular stockholders. Although not a stockholder or director, Will stood outside the lodge and overheard the discussion.

There was a resolution proffered by a man Will didn't know to divorce the association from the camp meeting. He claimed the camp meeting this year was a failure and would lead people to believe Rehoboth was also a failure as a watering place. Other voices not recognized by Will expressed concerns that Rehoboth was falling behind Cape May and Ocean City in development, particularly now that the railroad had been extended to Ocean City. Others grumbled about the restrictions on amusements that the conference placed on the association, such as prohibiting dancing, card-playing, and tenpins.

Rev. Quigg countered these claims by pointing out that this season's camp was well-attended and the Surf House and cottages were nearly full all summer. He also noted it was likely the Junction and Breakwater rail line would be extended to Rehoboth by next summer and bring more church folks to the camp meeting. Will didn't hear Mr. Bright take a position on disconnecting the camp from the rest of the town. Instead, Bright described the large hotel he planned to build on the oceanfront at Surf and Delaware Avenues by next season.

Quigg's face was ashen as he emerged from the preachers' lodge. He came looking for Will.

"Reverend Todd and Bishop Scott would be heartbroken if they heard what I just did in there," he said in a low but angry voice. "I'm afraid the new shareholders and directors not connected to the church want to change the vision that Reverend Todd had for Rehoboth. We all need to keep our noses clean and not give the conference reasons to abandon Rehoboth as a camp meeting place."

The next morning, Rev. Quigg summoned Will into the preachers' lodge. "Reverend Thompson, I understand you've been spending time in our organist's tent and at her home in Lewes.

Campers see that. It doesn't look good for the conference or the camp meeting leadership."

"She's frightened to be here alone with her son. I've behaved properly and never been with her alone in her tent or at her home," Will explained, realizing he was shading the truth.

"I hear rumors she's been with a lot of men."

"That's not fair," Will countered, his voice rising and the veins in his neck beginning to protrude. "She's a good Christian woman, and those rumors are just idle gossip. You and I both know what the scriptures say about gossipers and busybodies."

"Regardless, the appearance is not lost on the other preachers and campers," said Quigg, who obviously was still angry about the shareholders' meeting the day before. "You can't let your ministry be undermined by indiscretion. As a director of the association and the presiding elder of the Wilmington district, I can't just look the other way."

Will nodded and vowed to himself not to go in Susanna's tent again. At least not while Quigg was there.

Chapter Twenty-Seven

HUNTING

May 1876

"I'VE PUT UP two thousand in stock for the extension of the rail line from Lewes to the Rehoboth campground," announced President William Bright to the association directors gathered at two of the twenty-two tables in the dining room of his new hotel located at Surf and Delaware Avenues. "The Junction and Breakwater needs us to pony up twenty grand, which will be one-third of the total cost. Who else will step up with me to help fund this worthwhile venture?"

Will sat in a fancy Windsor chair next to his brother at a nearby table in the Bright House's spacious dining room. The hotel was a magnificent four-story structure with a decorative mansard roof, wooden columns, a huge porch overlooking the Atlantic, and an American flag flying from the rooftop. In addition to the large, well-appointed dining room and parlor on the first floor, there were fifty-seven guest rooms on the upper floors. The framing and woodwork were done in Wilmington, shipped to Lewes by rail, and hauled by teams to Rehoboth. The Bright House was due to open on July first with Mrs. Annie Grubb, who managed hotels in Wilmington, as the proprietress.

Bright House Hotel (from May 1877, Rehoboth Beacon, courtesy of Rehoboth Beach Museum

Bright had hired George to oversee construction of the hotel over the winter even though he had offered the job to Will three years earlier. Will was disappointed that Bright had not even had the courtesy to talk to him about it. He was getting paid the paltry sum of two dollars a week for his service at Bethel Church and three dollars a week for overseeing the association's improvements and lot sales. Meanwhile, George was getting twenty dollars a week working for Bright. Hotel construction had been delayed due to an economic recession in 1873 and Bright's unsuccessful bid for governor the following year. Will wondered if his close connection to the conference as a local preacher had changed Bright's mind about who to involve in his business.

"Billy, I'll invest a thousand and then build connecting railways on Rehoboth and Surf Avenues," Director J.J. McCullough boldly offered. Several other directors made more modest proposals but agreed to enlist their business colleagues to purchase stock in the railroad extension. Rev. Quigg advised those gathered that efforts were being made to have a large camp meeting in July, and circulars had been sent to all the preachers on the Delmarva Peninsula.

Bright had arranged for an excursion train from Wilmington that morning to bring more than 200 of his friends, business colleagues, and the association's directors to the grand opening of the Bright House. A four-course dinner had been served midday followed by the association's meeting, which ended in time for the directors to catch hacks waiting outside the hotel to take them back to Lewes for the 6 p.m. train.

As the directors' meeting ended, George gave Will a tour of the hotel, boasting about how he had to crack the whip on the local carpenters to get the work finished in time. They ended up on the porch watching the gentle waves break on the shoreline in front of them. Bright came over to George and warmly greeted him with a handshake. He nodded at Will but did not extend his hand.

"You did a first-rate job superintending the construction of my hotel," Bright said as he removed a cigar from the inside pocket of his suit coat and offered one to George. Will could see the same amber glass flask he noticed three years earlier tucked in the pocket of Bright's suit coat. "Let's have some supper and discuss how you can help me this summer." Bright escorted George to a private table in the corner of the dining room, leaving Will on the porch to ponder what George would be doing for Bright.

THE CAMP MEETING opened on July twenty-first with Bishop Scott attending for only one day and very few other ministers in attendance. As a result, Will had to lead at least one of the services every other day. The Dover district's presiding elder, Rev. Hough, took charge of the camp, and Rev. Quigg was noticeably absent. Only thirty-five of the sixty tents were occupied.

Will saw Rev. Todd only briefly at the annual conference meeting as he now was assigned to the church in Easton, Maryland and no longer made the journey to Rehoboth for the camp meetings. Will assumed Todd participated in a camp meeting elsewhere on the Peninsula, but he worried that his mentor had lost interest in Rehoboth.

Meanwhile, the Surf and Bright hotels were brimming over with vacationers from Wilmington and Baltimore. The cottages, including eight new ones built for $600-$1,000 each, also were full. Steamers carried visitors from New York and Philadelphia to the pier in Lewes, where hacks ferried them to and from Rehoboth.

Lewes Steamship Pier (undated, courtesy of Lewes Historical Society).

While some of the boarders at the Surf House attended the camp meeting services in the grove, Will noticed that more were interested in bathing in the ocean and observing charades, tableaux, and readings in the parlor of the Surf House. He heard from others about dancing, drinking, and card playing at the Bright House, but he chose to stay away.

Will saw very little of his brother, who no longer attended services at Bethel or served as a warden at the tabernacle. When Will encountered George on the boardwalk one evening, his brother told him he was too busy working for Mr. Bright to be religious.

As had become the custom, the annual meeting of association shareholders took place while the camp was in session. With Mr. Bright presiding as president, the meeting was held at his hotel. It was decided at the meeting that any lot-holder could become a stockholder of one share in the association provided he erected a $500 house on his lot and that all payments on the lot had been made. It was further resolved that two-thirds of the association's directors must be members of the Methodist-Episcopal Church. Will wondered if the increase in stockholders would give Bright and others on the board enough votes to change some of the camp meeting rules established by the conference.

There also was a discussion about whether persons should be allowed to erect tenpin alleys and billiard tables on the association's grounds. Most of the shareholders favored permitting this, but Rev. Stevenson from Baltimore reminded those gathered that the association's charter, which didn't permit any activity inconsistent with Christian morality as defined by the Methodist-Episcopal Church, would not allow the board to approve such amusements for use by the public. Will noticed that Rev. Martindale from Wilmington was the only minister elected to the nine-member board of directors, and Rev. Quigg did not attend the annual meeting.

SUSANNA CONTINUED TO play for the camp meetings and at Bethel Church. Will and Matthew became closer at the camp and when Will visited Susanna's home on Sundays after church. During planting and harvesting season, Will brought Matthew to his farm to help Luke and him with the heavy lifting. Will taught Matthew how to load and fire his shotgun, and Matthew expressed a strong interest in learning how to hunt waterfowl.

With Susanna's encouragement, Will took Matthew one early October morning to a secluded area owned by his distant Thompson relatives on the edge of Rehoboth Bay. This was a popular place for hunters staying nearby at Captain Tredenick's boarding house in Rehoboth City. After baiting an adjacent field with corn, Will and Matthew retreated to a pine thicket bordering the bay to wait for the migrating Canadian geese to pitch in.

Will heard other hunters occasionally firing from some of the blinds around the bay. He filled his old muzzleloader with black powder and steel shot and handed it to Matthew, telling the boy not to stand. They hunched down in their open blind to hide and wait. They could hear honking in the distance that was getting louder. As the geese swooped in from the bay to feast on the corn, Matthew excitedly stood up to aim. Will heard several booms from just behind them. Before Will could say or do anything, Matthew slumped down in a heap beside him, his right arm bleeding profusely through his flannel shirt.

Will quickly pulled out his handkerchief and made a tourniquet that he wrapped around Matthew's arm to try to stop the bleeding. Matthew was semi-conscious and began to moan. Will dragged the boy to his horse, lifted him into the saddle, and jumped on Gideon while holding the boy with one arm. Will urged Gideon into a gallop, and they headed up the road to Lewes and straight to Doctor Hall's office.

The doctor examined Matthew's wounds, injected morphine into his left arm to ease the pain, and cleaned and wrapped his wounds with cotton sheeting. He pulled Will aside. "The boy's going to survive, but I think there's some buckshot lodged in his upper arm that I'm not equipped to remove. It probably can stay there, but he may experience some paralysis. You can take him home now. If he continues to have a lot of pain, bring him back and I'll give him another injection."

Matthew was now fully awake, and Will explained to him that he'd been shot by unknown hunters firing behind them when he raised up to shoot. Will felt he was partly responsible for not realizing there were other hunters in their midst and not forcing Matthew to stay down. He decided to spare the boy those details at least for now and took him to Susanna's home.

"Oh my God, what happened?" Susanna screamed when she saw Matthew with his arm wrapped and dangling limply at his side.

He told her everything, including what Dr. Hall said about the buckshot in his arm and the boy's prognosis. "It was an accident. I'm sorry," Will said sadly, knowing that Matthew had disobeyed his direction to stay down.

"Well, right now it looks like his right arm is useless!" she wailed. "Will Thompson, how could you let this happen to my only child?"

"I'm sorry. How can I help?"

"Just go, and leave us alone," Susanna said, pointing to the door.

Chapter Twenty-Eight

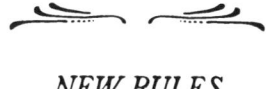

NEW RULES

March 1877

WILL LISTENED INTENTLY to Rev. Piersen give a report from the Special Committee on Camp Meetings. It was the last day of the annual gathering of Methodist-Episcopal ministers in the Wilmington Conference being held at Milford's church. He was joined at the dais by Rev. Brown and Rev. Parsons, senior pastors of two large churches in the Wilmington district who also were members of the Special Committee. Rev. Piersen reported thirty-eight communications received from quarterly meetings of conference pastors, many finding evils associated with the camp meetings that needed to be corrected.

"Desecration of the Sabbath by traffic and travel," Piersen said, reading from his prepared statement. "Needless self-indulgences by extravagant outfit and luxurious living, and the temptation too often yielded to by preachers to exhibit their own intellect and culture rather than the simplicity and power of the Gospel." He paced as he read. "There is a worldliness of spirit, which fills the tents with companies of merry men and women and leaves the prayer circle empty and sad. All of these evils combine to prevent large success in saving souls and even result in utter failures."

Rev. Pierson explained that some of the pastors at the quarterly conferences were in favor of ceasing camp meetings altogether, while most agreed to continue them with strict rules of order to include meeting on only one Sabbath with no Sunday traffic or railroad travel permitted. In addition, he reported, the Special Committee was recommending that preachers refuse to attend any camp meeting that did not include in its printed regulation prohibitions against all buying and selling on the Sabbath, photograph galleries, promenading, and loud conversations and social visiting in the tents during the religious services. The ordained pastors attending passed a resolution adopting these camp meeting requirements as well as a resolution advising all ministers and members to abstain from the use of tobacco, injurious as it was to both soul and body.

Will was shaken by the presentation and wondered how it would affect the Rehoboth camp meeting. Rev. Todd sat down next to him for the final dinner at the conference. "What do you make of the new camp meetin' requirements?" Will asked the pastor.

"I agree we need to set some rules. Many of the camp meetings are looking more like county fairs with hucksters and politicians diverting the attention of the faithful. Some of our brethren are showing off their preaching skills to get applause from those gathered. That's not what the camp meetings are meant to be as you'll recall from the Zoar meeting several years ago."

"What about Rehoboth? I noticed you didn't attend last summer."

Todd paused to clear his throat and pulled a handkerchief from inside his suit coat. "I'm concerned about what I started there. I hear that Mr. Bright's new hotel on the grounds is drawing many people for amusements that are inconsistent with the practices of our church. What are you seeing?"

"Some folks would rather stay and eat at Bright's fancy hotel or at the Surf House than tent in the grove," Will said as he looked down at his plate of food, not wanting to say too much.

"I'm afraid when the railroad gets extended from Lewes, that'll bring a slew of sinners to Rehoboth and be the death knell for the camp meetings there," Todd prophesized. "Reverend Quigg won't be able to gather enough votes to prevent disagreeable changes to the association's charter."

"I'll do all I can to prevent that from happenin'," Will said boldly without thinking how he could accomplish that.

"I'd appreciate that, Will. Rehoboth is such a beautiful place for a camp meeting and for our members to be renewed spiritually. I hear from Reverend Pegg that Susanna Robinson is no longer attending Bethel and playing the organ there."

"It's because of her son," Will said. "He was hurt in a huntin' accident. She holds me responsible and doesn't want to see me preach or talk to me at Bethel. I hear she's attendin' St. Peter's in Lewes and playin' the organ there."

"Is the boy going to be all right?"

"He took some buckshot in his right arm. Last I saw, he couldn't use it."

"Sorry to hear that. Have you talked with her about playing at the Rehoboth camp meeting this summer?"

"Not really. Every time I stop by to see her, she acts like I'm a stranger and tells me she's too busy to talk."

"How are your own kids doing?"

"Both of the twins got married last year and moved out to be with their husbands. Mary lives in Lewes with the new doctor's son, and Hannah married a farmer from Milton. Ruth and Luke are still with me but are lookin' to buy some land and start their own farm."

"And Willie?" Rev. Todd asked.

Will took a deep breath, exhaled, and slumped down haplessly in his chair, head in hands. "Nothin'."

"You've been through a lot in the last couple of years," Rev. Todd offered with a compassionate grimace on his face. He blew his nose into his handkerchief and leaned back in his chair. "You may not know this, but I've had my own family troubles." Will raised his head and looked at Todd, who lowered his voice. "My oldest son never came back from in the war. We don't know if he's dead or alive, and my youngest daughter has been an invalid since she was a child. Taking care of her is a full-time job for my wife. And as you can see, I'm still suffering from severe bronchitis."

"I didn't realize. You always seem so cheerful. How do you do it?"

"Sometimes I feel poor in spirit and almost without hope. We can't always understand why things happen as they do. But I seek peace in knowing that my Lord and Savior Jesus Christ understands my circumstances and is always present to bring me healing and comfort. Don't lose hope, Will. You're doing God's work at Bethel and the camp meeting in Rehoboth. Don't you agree?"

Will nodded and felt a sense of relief, though this was quickly followed by guilt for taking solace in his mentor's problems.

Chatper Twenty-Nine

INSPECTION

July 1877

REHOBOTH WAS BUSTLING with many visitors from Wilmington, Baltimore, Philadelphia, New York, and Washington, D.C.

The grove had fewer than fifty tent houses occupied, while the Bright House was full and holding hops with orchestras and dancing on Friday and Saturday nights. A large stable had been constructed next to the Bright so those lodging there could rent a horse and carriage to take a delightful drive along the hard-packed ocean beach.

The Surf House accommodated mostly Baltimoreans looking for a quieter vacation. Preachers from Baltimore would conduct Sunday morning services in the parlor. Praise meetings were held in the evenings where a talented young woman from Baltimore played sing-along gospel songs on Mrs. Martin's organ, accompanying the beautiful voice of May Taggart of Wilmington.

Farther south in Rehoboth City, the new Douglass House hosted several dozen of Delaware's state senators and representatives, who enjoyed sailing on Rehoboth Bay and strolling along the sandy beach. After dinner, the "Legislative Glee Club" assembled in the parlor of the Douglass. There, they entertained the audience with "Sweet By-and-By," "Shoo Fly," and other vocal gems. At midnight, an unnamed number of attendees repaired to the beach to indulge in a "buck" bath for nearly half an hour.

Only a handful of preachers from the conference came to the camp meetings for short stints. Susanna was absent and had rebuffed all of Will's attempts to apologize. Rev. Quigg attended the association's annual meeting and preached one service before leaving for Dover. As a result, Will had to fill in at the preachers' platform for many services that suffered without Susanna's inspirational organ music. With no warden to patrol the grounds, Will tried his best to ensure that the conference's rules were observed.

One Saturday afternoon between services, Will led ten of the older children from the camp on a walk along the beach to observe the Cape Henlopen lighthouse five miles north of the camp meeting grounds. Because his bad right leg was becoming stiffer with age, Will rode in a carriage he rented from the Bright for fifty cents. As they reached the lighthouse, they climbed up the twenty-five-foot dune, and Will knocked on the door of the lighthouse keeper's cottage. After some time, the door opened and a bleary-eyed middle-aged man came out to greet the group. He introduced himself as Mr. Joseph.

Cape Henlopen Lighthouse and Keeper's House (undated, courtesy of Lewes Historical Society).

"I'm sorry to keep you waiting. I was up most of the night tending the candles up here and in the Beacon light a mile north of here," he said motioning to the adjacent Cape Henlopen lighthouse. "The keeper there has been out sick with malaria."

"I'm Reverend Thompson from Bethel church and, if you have the time, these kids from the Rehoboth camp meetin' would enjoy hearin' about the history of these lighthouses."

"I'd be happy to, pastor. The lower part of this structure was built by the English in seventeen-sixty-seven to get ships around the treacherous shoals of the Cape at night and during storms. It was mostly destroyed by the English in the Revolutionary War as they tried to get up the Delaware River to Wilmington and Philadelphia."

Some of the kids started fidgeting and yawning, so the keeper decided to shorten his presentation. "After the war, it was rebuilt to a height of seventy feet with a tube four inches in diameter at the top that's lit by a wick supplied with lard oil. Surrounding the tube is a solid silver reflector and circular magnifying glass made in Paris that cost fourteen thousand. We recently added a foghorn. You're welcome to come take a look."

Three of the older boys climbed up the circular staircase with the keeper to examine the inside of the structure and its expensive illumination apparatus. Two of the younger boys started wrestling on the beach, and Will had to break up the tussle. Mr. Joseph pointed to the lighthouse up the beach about a mile away.

"The Beacon light was built in eighteen twenty-four. It's forty-five feet high and is a similar design. Sometimes, I need to tend to both of them at night, making sure the wicks stay lit and the reflector is clean. I could use some help, if any of you's looking for a job." Joseph winked at Will.

There were no volunteers, and Will thanked the lightkeeper for his information and tour. The group journeyed back to Rehoboth, picking up unique conch and other shells as they walked. Arriving back at the Bright House, Will pointed out two dolphins skipping in and out of the sea just beyond the breakers.

Will returned to the grove and was met by two men in preachers' suits who had just arrived by carriage from Lewes. They introduced themselves as Rev. Johns and Rev. Green from Wilmington and said they were sent by the conference to inspect camp meetings in Kent, Sussex, and Wicomico Counties.

"Do you have room to board us in the preachers' lodge tonight?" asked Rev. Johns.

"That should be no problem. It's over there," said Will, pointing to the large tent behind the preachers' platform. "There aren't many preachers here this year so there's plenty of room. How long are you here for?"

"We'll watch tonight's service and stay for your Sunday morning service before heading to Zoar tomorrow night," said Rev. Green. "We'd like to see the rest of the grounds and maybe some local natural scenery tomorrow afternoon if there's time."

"You're welcome to preach tonight's service if you'd like," offered Will.

"Oh, no. We're tired from our journey," said Rev. Johns.

"I'm sure you have someone lined up to preach, and we wouldn't want to disappoint him," said Rev. Green.

Will excused himself and returned to the preachers' lodge to prepare his sermon for the evening service as the new arrivals strolled around the grove, inspecting the grounds and talking with the campers. The recent rains brought hordes of mosquitoes to the campground and the evening service wasn't well attended, as the locals and some of the campers in the grove chose to walk down to the Surf House to hear the dramatic readings and organ music. Fighting off the biting pests, Will gave his Zoar Road testimony and tied it to the Prodigal Son parable, but no worshippers came down the sawdust trail to be baptized or accept Jesus as their savior.

On Sunday morning, the service again was lightly attended as a local preacher from Georgetown tried his best to exhort those attending with an altar call. But it was to no avail. Will watched as the two preachers from Wilmington made notes and whispered to each other.

"If you're hungry, I have some stew I can heat up over the campfire," Will offered them.

"We'd appreciate that," said Rev. Green. "Afterwards, could we see the rest of the association's grounds?"

Will provided dinner to the visiting preachers, and then all three walked down Rehoboth Avenue to the ocean. They visited the Surf House, where guests were enjoying the ocean breeze on the front porch and listening to secular organ music emanating from the parlor. Young adults and older children were playing croquet in the backyard while a huckster from Lewes sold ice cream from his wagon on Virginia Avenue. The preachers made notes of these activities.

The threesome then proceeded south on Surf Avenue to the Bright House, where young women wearing revealing bathing costumes were sunning themselves on the beach. They went into the parlor of the Bright House and saw musical instruments lying in the corner.

"Take a look at this," said Rev. Johns, motioning for Rev. Green to come and see a flyer posted on the wall by the stairway. "They had a dance here last night."

Will could smell smoke and alcohol in the parlor and wondered if the two Wilmington preachers noticed. They inhaled and made more notes.

"Would you like to see some of the natural beauty around here?" Will asked.

"Yes, indeed," said Rev. Green.

Will led them walking to the head of Rehoboth Bay, where an old Indian cemetery was hidden among a lush forest of white oaks, swamp maples, and loblolly pines. Just beyond the forest was an open meadow and salt marsh, a popular trapping spot for deer, muskrat, possum, and rabbit. Will hoped the Wilmington pastors might see some of these game.

However, as they entered the meadow, they heard a voice crying out for help. Will hobbled through the knee-high grass to find a young man with his ankle caught in a muskrat trap. Will studied the man's copper-toned face and high cheekbones and shouted to the pastors that the trapped man was a Nanticoke Indian. He called for the pastors to assist, but they held back.

"Please, I need your help over here," Will implored.

"How do you know that Indian won't hurt or rob us?" Rev. Green asked with a trembling voice. "We need to get back to the campground, pack our things, and be on our way to Zoar," Green called over his shoulder as the two Wilmington pastors quickly headed back into the forest to retrace their steps.

With great effort, Will was able to free the Nanticoke from the trap, but his ankle was badly cut and swollen, making it impossible for him to walk. Will had the Nanticoke put his arm over Will's left shoulder so they had two good legs to limp through the woods and back to the campground. On the way, Will learned that the Nanticoke man had come to visit the sacred burial ground and pray for those buried there using the Nanticoke's version of the Lord's Prayer.

As they approached the campground, Will recalled that one of the campers was a doctor from Baltimore. He took the Nanticoke to the doctor's tent as the Wilmington pastors watched from afar and then departed in a carriage for Zoar.

Chapter Thirty

ISAAC

July 1878

WILL COULD HEAR the train whistle blow and smell the burning coal of the engine from his farm. The J&B extension from Lewes to Rehoboth was now complete, and the association had donated two acres to the railroad to build its new depot at the entrance to the campground. Each day two trains from Wilmington made the five-and-a-half-hour trip.

"You know, little brother, this town is goin' to explode now that the railroad is here," George yelled to Will from the platform as the steam engine with five cars pulled into the depot on the first day of the camp meeting.

Will nodded to George, who he had not talked to in two years, as he greeted the new camp meeting arrivals carrying their Bibles and bags through the fence gate to the grove. The association had appointed Will superintendent of this year's camp meeting, for which he was paid an extra ten dollars above his local preacher salary of one hundred dollars per year. As superintendent, Will was in charge of all operations at the grove, including tent house rentals, food supplies, and enforcement of the camp meeting rules set by the conference.

He checked his notebook and directed the reserved renters to their tent houses while handing them a printed copy of the camp meeting regulations and schedule. For those asking about the Surf House, Will gestured toward the ocean and recommended they engage one of the waiting hacks. He handed them his printed paper and encouraged them to come back to the camp meeting services in the grove.

Meanwhile, George held a "Bright House" sign and pointed the more well-to-do arrivals to Mr. Metcalf's stage waiting to take them to the Bright. He helped load their large Saratoga trunks onto the stage and handed them a printed schedule of activities planned for their stay at the Bright.

As three people boarded the train for its departure back to Lewes and ultimately Wilmington, George strolled over to Will, who was checking his notebook.

"How's it look for your camp meetin' this summer?" George asked.

"Not great," Will said. Less than half of the tent houses had been rented for the week, and few preachers had committed to come.

"I think the camp meetin' idea has run its course," George said.

"Folks want to come to Rehoboth to get a break from city life and have a good time. They don't need to hear a bunch of preachin'."

Will breathed deeply and hoped his brother's brusque assessment was wrong. "What's goin' on at the Bright?" asked Will. "Are you holdin' hops and servin' malts and whiskey?"

"We run a tight ship. We don't sell any alcohol or schedule any dancin' but we can't control what our payin' guests bring with them or organize. Mr. Bright's the president of the association and knows and follows the rules," George declared as if he had rehearsed it.

Will twisted his face and raised an eyebrow. "That's not what I hear, nor what I've seen. How much is Bright payin' you?"

George ignored the question. "Is that pretty blonde organist goin' be playin' for you this year?"

"It's none of your business. You don't go to Bethel anymore, and I don't need or want you hangin' around the campground. I have work to do." Will abruptly turned his back on George, closed the gate, and limped to the preachers' lodge.

AFTER WILL HELPED free the Nanticoke from the trap and brought him back to the campground, he learned his name was Isaac Hill. Will and Isaac spent time together until his ankle healed enough to go home. Will was surprised to discover that Isaac lived nearby and was a member of Israel Methodist Episcopal Church located just west of Lewes.

Isaac explained that his Uncle John Hill was the local preacher at the small Israel church that was attended by Nanticokes and African Americans. Although he knew the Israel church was considered part of Bethel's charge that included a few other small country churches, Will had never been there. He was amazed when Isaac asked to borrow his Bible and found him reading it and making notes every day.

Isaac explained how the Nanticokes had lived along the Nanticoke River in western Sussex County for hundreds of years before the English settled here. They came to the Rehoboth area in the summer and fall to hunt and fish and then returned to their inland tent homes for the winter. Will had invited Isaac to return to this year's camp meeting and was surprised but pleased to see him approach the gate.

"Welcome back, Isaac. It's really good to see you again," Will said. "How's your ankle?"

"It's all healed up. I'm fine thanks to you and the doctor. I'd like to invite my Uncle John Hill to a service if that's okay. He's the local preacher at our Israel church."

"I'll check with Reverend Quigg when he gets here. I'm sure it'll be fine."

"I'd like to return the grace you showed me last summer," said Isaac. "How can I help out at the camp meeting?"

"How 'bout if you walk around the campground and let me

know if you see any alcohol, cards, gamblin', dancin', or loud conversations?"

"Yes, Reverend, I'll keep an eye out for those evils and report any I see to you right away."

"Here, wear this." Will handed Isaac his old warden's badge. "We'll pay you for your services."

"That's not necessary. I'm just happy to be here and take in the good preaching and prayer meetings."

"Bishop Scott is due to arrive this afternoon with his son, who's also a Methodist-Episcopal preacher. I hope you get to meet the bishop and he's in good enough health to preach. They built the tent house over there," Will said, pointing to the two-story structure on the opposite side of the tabernacle.

"WE'LL NEED TO hold the meeting in the tabernacle," President Bright said to the directors as he surveyed more than fifty stockholders who showed up for the annual meeting of the association five days after the camp meeting opened. "The preachers' lodge ain't big enough anymore. It looks like the new shareholders have something to tell us," he said with a smile.

Will sat in the back row of the tabernacle to observe the proceedings. He looked around and noticed that the new stockholders who had purchased lots and built cottages weren't the familiar faces from past camp meetings.

Bright gave an update on improvements added to the association's grounds since last year. He related that there were ten new cottages, a modern train depot, and a new annex to the Bright House where telegraph service was now available for businessmen to stay in touch with their affairs. He noted that the Company C military band from Wilmington would be playing at the Surf House this summer, and that the Sunday School Convention with hundreds of children was scheduled for next month.

Five new directors were elected to make up the ten-member board, only two of whom were ministers. Rev. Quigg was present and indicated he had no interest in running for the board but would continue to serve as chair of the Committee on Order, which set and enforced the association's rules of conduct.

Dr. Caldwell, chairman of the committee from the Sunday School Convention, raised his hand and asked to speak. "I have on good authority that there is dancing, card-playing, and alcohol being served at Mr. Bright's hotel," declared Caldwell, who was seated next to Quigg. "My convention has passed a resolution recognizing such practices as contrary to the charter of this association and the discipline of the Methodist Episcopal Church and request that the stockholders and directors take immediate action to remedy these evils."

"In fact, I understand a hop is planned for this evening at the Bright!" Rev. Quigg shouted, jumping up from his seat. "All of these sins are prohibited by the church and the charter of this association. Therefore, I propose a resolution that the Committee on Order and any of its members be instructed to expel from these grounds anyone guilty of violating the rules of the association, and that a notice of this determination be posted on the grounds."

After much discussion, Will was surprised the resolution passed by those stockholders in attendance. Rev. Quigg and Dr. Caldwell were nodding and smiling once the vote was tallied. They came over to Will to discuss how he needed to police the downtown establishments and post notices.

"The association has no legal basis to enforce its rules against the visitors at the Bright House or any other private establishment," declared Mr. Betts, a lawyer from Georgetown who had just been elected to the board and was seated next to Bright. "Mr. Bright and his proprietors can't control what their guests bring with them or plan for amusement. Dancing is even occurring at the association's Surf House. The association should limit its concerns to what goes on there and at the camp meetings, where I understand liquor, poker, and euchre are enjoyed in the tents on this very ground."

Will felt an anvil drop in the pit of his stomach as Rev. Quigg turned and stared at him.

He hadn't seen any of what the lawyer claimed. Where did he get his information? He needed to talk to Isaac.

Chapter Thirty-One

REVELATION

"I'VE BEEN DOING my job. I swear on my Bible that I haven't seen any liquor or cards," said Isaac when Will confronted him that afternoon. "There was a burly man smoking a cigar here yesterday looking around while you were preaching. He opened the screen doors of some of the tent houses and looked inside. I asked him who he was and what he was doing. He told me he used to be a warden and was looking for some old friends. Someone saw him and called him George."

Will jumped on Gideon and raced to the Bright House, where he found his brother rearranging the furniture in the parlor to make a large open space surrounded by chairs. At one end of the room, musical instruments were positioned on a small wooden stage surrounding a piano. Four men sat at a table in the corner playing poker while smoking cigars and drinking whiskey.

Seeing the piano brought memories of Elizabeth, Willie, and Susanna flooding back to Will. But this was no time for that. He grabbed George's shoulder from behind and turned him around. "I just heard you were at the campground yesterday doin' Bright's dirty work. You stay away from there or I'll have you arrested for trespassin'."

"Hey, hey, little brother. You better be careful who you're accusin' of what. I told you before, we can't control what our guests do any more than you can control what your campers do in their tents. Face it. Your holy rollers will end up somewhere else, and this hotel and ones like it are goin' to take over Rehoboth. The handwriting's on the wall."

"I'm not givin' up on the camp meetin' here just yet," said Will. "We've got a lot of soul savin' to do."

"That's a joke. I'm Mr. Bright's right-hand man, and he pays me very well," George said, holding his head high. "You should get on board with the resort business here. Otherwise move to Lewes and be closer to Bethel, where all you got is a part-time preacher job. I knew when we was growin' up you'd never amount to nothin'."

Will's face reddened, and he could feel the veins in his neck bulging. He wanted to punch his brother in the face. But he remembered what Rev. Todd told him after George ridiculed him and kicked him in the face at the camp meeting five years earlier. Will turned and saw Isaac standing on the porch listening to his exchange with George. He paused and pondered whether to turn the other cheek.

Will mounted Gideon and left before he did something he would regret. When he returned to the campground, he reported what he had seen at the Bright to Rev. Quigg and explained that his brother had been snooping in the campers' tent houses the day before.

"I'm prepared to take care of Mr. Bright and his dirty tactics," Quigg said to Will. He retreated to the horse pound and returned with a uniformed marshal and a man in a suit. "Will, tell this marshal and our lawyer, Mr. Day, what you saw this afternoon."

Will recounted what he had seen. He led them down Rehoboth Avenue to the Bright House, where the marshal stood guard on the boardwalk in front of the hotel with Mr. Day. George came out to investigate and, after consulting with Mr. Bright, advised them there would be no dance that night because the piano player was ill.

IT WAS A HOT and humid August day in Dover. Will could feel the white shirt under his preacher's jacket was soaked as he entered the courthouse with Mr. Day and Rev. Quigg. They had come by carriage from Lewes the day before and spent the night in Frederica with the family of the pastor of Barratt's Chapel. They left Frederica at dawn for the dusty thirteen-mile trip to downtown Dover.

When they entered the Chancellor's ornate courtroom, Will saw his brother and Mr. Bright, as well as Mr. Burton, the Bright's lessee, sitting on the back row talking with a well-dressed man who looked like he could be a lawyer. Rev. Quigg had arranged for Mr. Dodd, one of the association's stockholders, to bring a suit in the Court of Chancery seeking an injunction against Mr. Burton to prohibit dancing at the Bright in violation of the association's charter. Will was called to the witness stand by Mr. Day to testify about what he had seen a month earlier.

"Mr. Thompson, did you observe anyone dancing at the Bright House?" asked Jacob Moore, Burton's attorney, on cross-examination.

"Well, no. But it was clear they were preparin' for a hop that evenin', and I've seen flyers posted at the Bright advertisin' upcomin' dances."

"Do you know if those dances were ever held?"

"I heard they were."

"Did you observe Mr. Burton or anyone working for him at the Bright House serving alcohol or providing playing cards?" asked Moore.

"Well, no. Not actually."

"So would you agree that the men may have brought their own alcohol and cards with them?"

"That's possible," Will allowed.

"And is it not also possible that those attending the religious services at the campground may have brought alcohol and cards with them?"

"That's very unlikely."

The Chancellor dismissed Will from the witness stand and called the lawyers up to the bench for a conversation that Will could not hear. Mr. Day came back to Will and advised that the hearing was being postponed in hopes that the dispute could be worked out.

Rev. Quigg had very little to say during the carriage ride back to Lewes, but Will could tell the minister was very disappointed. Day tried to explain that obtaining an injunction against a business was always very difficult, especially in this case, where the charter's language didn't expressly prohibit dancing.

SIX WEEKS LATER, George showed up at Will's farmhouse holding a piece of paper.

"Here's a message for you we just received at the Bright. You might want to read it little brother, and follow what it says." George handed Will the telegram.

It was from Rev. Quigg advising Will that the board of directors had changed the name of the association. "The new name is the Rehoboth Beach Association STOP Change all signs and flyers to conform to the new name STOP"

Will hung his head as he realized that Rehoboth would no longer be identified as a Methodist Episcopal camp meeting location.

"You've lost, little brother," George said with a smirk. "Time for you to get a real job."

Will looked up at his brother. "You've never liked me, have you? Why is that?"

"Maybe it's time you knew the truth if you really want to."

"What do ya mean?"

"You ain't really a Thompson like me," George said with a haughty chuckle. "Your father was a Nanticoke from over near Millsboro."

These words dumbfounded Will. He stood with his mouth open not knowing what to say. Finally, he asked, "How do you know that?"

"My father told me after our mother died and asked me never to tell another soul. But now he and our mother are gone, it don't matter anymore."

Will tried to take this in. He always wondered why he and George looked so different. George was a much bigger man like his father and had a ruddy complexion with straight reddish-blonde hair and different facial features. Will always figured he took more after his mother, with his copper-toned skin, black hair, and high cheekbones.

"Why are you tellin' me this now?"

"I figured it was time you knew why I'm a better man than you."

Will's anger boiled up. He took a deep breath. "Who else knows about this?"

"I don't 'spect no one else knows, unless your real father is still livin'. I decided you needed to know why you's such a failure and always will be. That's why my father gave me the family farmhouse and land and you got only a little piece and the slave's shanty."

Will felt betrayed. He vaguely remembered from his early childhood a man they called "the Indian" who worked on the farm and stayed with his family in the tiny house that Will inherited. Unanswered questions flooded his mind. Where was "the Indian" now, and what was his real name? Did he have any half-brothers and sisters? What ancestry did his father have? Nanticoke? African? White? A mixture? He pondered whether it was good to know any of this.

George mounted his horse to leave, looking down at his brother, whose face was bowed with eyes closed. "I hate to be the one to tell you this."

After a long silence, Will looked up at George. "No, you don't."

Chapter Thirty-Two

THE INVITATION

March 1879

THE WIND HOWLED off the Delaware River as the stage pulled up to the Methodist Episcopal Church in New Castle. Will and Rev. England from Bethel had taken the train from Lewes to Wilmington for the annual conference. There was still a layer of snow visible on the ground as the team's hooves clop clopped on the cobblestone streets in old town New Castle.

Will was anxious to find Rev. Todd and relate what George had told him five months earlier. His brother's claim about their different fathers had consumed his thinking. How could he know if it was true or if George was just making it up to have something else to lord over him? And yet his body type and visage were so different from his father and brother.

In the past month, Will had displaced his initial anger against his parents and his brother to a place of questioning God. Why was he given this burden? And why now? He had not told Rev. England or anyone else because he was worried it might affect his position and acceptance within the Bethel community. But he believed he could tell Rev. Todd, who would understand and provide wise counsel.

Todd was busy organizing matters for the conference when Will arrived. After supper on the second day, Will was able to corner the senior pastor, and they found their way to the choir loft for some privacy. Will recounted what George had told him.

Rev. Todd took out his handkerchief to blow his nose. He cleared his throat and stroked his beard. "You know the scriptures teach us that we're all God's children if we believe in Jesus Christ. It doesn't matter the color of your skin or your facial features."

"I know they say that, but why would God hold this back from me until now?"

"Maybe you weren't in a place to handle it before. Remember that God's timing is perfect. It's our impatience and unbelief that get us into trouble."

Will ruminated on what he had just heard. Had he known of his ethnicity earlier, how might that have affected his life? Would he have married Elizabeth and had his family? Would he have met Rev. Todd and been born again? What if his father hadn't agreed to treat him as a son? Would he have been a slave working on a farm in Millsboro? His eyes full of tears, Will looked up at Rev. Todd. "How will this affect my ministry at Bethel and the Rehoboth camp meetin'?"

"I think it will make you a better pastor to advocate on behalf of those who are not yet fully accepted in our church culture. You can minister to the Negroes and the Nanticokes with a level of understanding and compassion that others can't."

Will recalled his friendships with Elijah and Isaac and nodded. "Thank you, Reverend Todd. I really needed to hear this. What should I do about George? He admits he hates me and is workin' against the camp meetings."

"George gives you an opportunity to show grace. Keep in mind, you aren't defined or valued by what George thinks about you. There's an upper story more important than that."

Will and Todd retreated down to the church altar, where they knelt next to each other and prayed. For the first time in five months, Will was able to get a good night's sleep.

WILL MET WITH Rev. Quigg in the Preacher's Lodge to plan for the camp meeting that would begin the next day. Quigg had been appointed the superintendent instead of Will who wondered if that was due to the unfortunate events of the prior summer.

"We need to increase the number of campers attending," Quigg emphasized to Will. "Less than half of the tent houses are rented, and it'll be a shame if Bishop Scott and Bishop Simpson are preaching to a handful of worshippers. The newspapers will deem the Rehoboth camp meeting a total failure."

"How can I help?" Will asked.

"I suspect those renting at the Bright are a lost cause. But let's try to get the folks staying at the Surf House to come to services. We also need to get the locals to come in for the day."

"Would you mind if I recruited some members of the Israel ME Church and the St. George AME Church in Pilottown to come hear Bishop Scott preach?" asked Will.

"That might help fill up the tabernacle," Quigg said, "but they'd need to sit behind the preacher's platform, as is the custom for coloreds attending our camp meetings."

"I'll see what I can do," said Will, though he wondered why Christians of different colors couldn't sit together.

The Bright and Surf House were full every night, and Rehoboth was bustling with new activity. Meat and vegetable markets had opened under the management of two Lewes merchants. Mr. Beebe tended an ice cream parlor on Rehoboth Avenue near the ocean. There was even a new gallery on Virginia Avenue available for family and individual photos.

Music, dancing, and card and chess playing occurred every night at the Bright House, where the governor and his family stayed for a week in early July. James Hooper, a duck cloth manufacturer from Baltimore, installed a tenpin alley on Surf Avenue and hosted his Sunday school class from Baltimore at a large tent next to his oceanfront home on Maryland Avenue.

Fishing and boating on Lake Gerar were popular pastimes for the vacationers.

Will jumped on Gideon and galloped to Lewes. First he went to the Israel Church and found Rev. John Hill officiating a funeral in an adjacent graveyard. After the mourners had departed, he approached Rev. Hill.

"I'm Reverend Thompson from Bethel Church. We met at the Rehoboth campground last summer, and I know your nephew Isaac."

"Yes, Isaac speaks highly of you. He and I were hoping to come down for a service later this week if that's acceptable. I know some white folks don't like to see Nanticokes at their camp meetings."

"I'd be honored if you and Isaac could come. Bishop Scott is supposed to preach tomorrow night at our openin' service, and it would be such a blessin' if you came and brought some more folks from your congregation. I'm sure it'll be fine with Reverend Quigg and Bishop Scott."

"I'll see who's interested. I've always wanted to hear the bishop preach."

Will jumped back on Gideon and headed to St. George AME Church in Pilottown. The church was empty, but Will felt goose bumps as he looked around and recalled Elijah's funeral there six years earlier. He rode Gideon down Pilottown Road to Rev. Miller's home, where he and Elizabeth had supper with the Millers after Elijah's funeral. Will rapped on the screen door.

"Who is it?" came the deep bass voice of Rev. Miller.

"It's Reverend Will Thompson from Bethel Church."

THE INVITATION

"What do you want?"

"I'd like to speak to you if you have a moment."

Rev. Miller came to the door and squinted through the screen at Will.

"Do I know you?"

"Yes, I was here with my wife attendin' your son Elijah's funeral."

"Oh yes, now I remember. You were involved in the camp meeting in Rehoboth."

"I still am. Since I met you, I've become a local preacher with Bethel Church in Lewes."

"So what do you want? That was a very sad day when I last laid eyes on you."

"I'd like to invite you and your congregation to come to the camp meetin' tomorrow night and hear our Bishop Scott preach."

"You know we're an AME church, and our folks don't associate with the white church."

"I remember what you told me about Reverend Allen and the split sixty years ago. But Bishop Scott was against slavery and would welcome colored people to his service."

"I don't know. I'll pray on it and see where the Lord leads."

Chapter Thirty-Three

SINNERS VS. SAINTS

ALL THE SEATS in the tabernacle were taken, and several dozen people were standing in the rear. The entire area behind the preacher's platform was filled with colored people, including Reverend Miller and Reverend Hill, with another fifty men and women standing behind them. It was one of the largest turnouts for a service in the history of the Rehoboth Camp Meeting.

Will spotted Rev. Todd coming out of the preachers' lodge just before the service began.

"My goodness, this large gathering is amazing," exclaimed Rev. Todd. "Reverend Quigg tells me you're largely responsible for it."

"I don't know about that," Will said. "I'm surprised to see you here."

"You may recall I got assigned to the Milton church by the conference for this year. One of my trustees said he was going to hear Bishop Scott tonight, and I came along to see how the Rehoboth camp meeting is faring. It looks like you're doing a great job, Reverend Thompson," Todd said with a big grin. "I've got to get up on the preacher's platform before the service starts."

Rev. Quigg opened the service by thanking all those who came. He introduced Bishop Scott, who got up slowly from his seat on the preacher's platform and stood beside the pulpit with no notes in his hand. His feebleness and failing health were evident, but he persevered to preach for over an hour on the need for unity in the church among all races and creeds of Christians, using Jesus' parable of the Good Samaritan as his scripture. Scott explained his own conversion that occurred at a prayer meeting led by black women. As he finished, he acknowledged Rev. Miller and Rev. Hill and invited them to join him on the preachers' platform. Will mused that it was as though the bishop wanted to make the most of this unique opportunity to teach the whites how to love their neighbors with different skin colors.

At the end of the sermon, Rev. Todd stood and led those gathered in a stirring baritone rendition of "Just As I Am." Dozens of men and women of all colors came down the sawdust trail to the altar to be baptized or receive hands-on prayer from the bishop, Quigg, and Todd. After the service, those of color seated behind the platform mingled with their white brothers and sisters before leaving to journey in the starlit night back to Lewes.

Later in the evening, Rev. Todd found Will talking with Isaac next to the preachers' lodge. Will introduced Isaac to Todd and explained how they met, including the recalcitrance of the Wilmington preachers.

"Glad to meet you Isaac," Todd said, extending his hand. "I've seen your Uncle John at some quarterly meetings. He's a fine Christian preacher. I'm sorry some of my brethren from Wilmington didn't treat you very well. Fortunately, Will was the Good Samaritan there to help you."

"He surely was. And he's told me about how you changed his life."

"It was our Lord and Savior who transformed Will. I just happened to be in the right place at the right time to remind him who he is and who he can be," said Todd. "And look how God is using Will to bring Christian brothers and sisters of all stripes together."

Todd turned to Will. "You were the hands and feet of Jesus encouraging the Israel and St. George's preachers and their congregants to come together tonight," Rev. Todd gushed as he slapped Will on the back. "You helped Rehoboth be room enough for all. How are you and your brother doing?"

Will thanked Todd for his compliments but didn't answer his question. He hadn't tried to talk with George since he and Todd met in New Castle back in March. He knew he had to fix that.

FIVE DAYS LATER, the stockholders of the association met in the tabernacle with Mr. Bright presiding. Directors Bright and William Hooper had encouraged like-minded stockholders from Wilmington and Baltimore to come to the meeting. They had gathered dozens of proxies from those not able to attend to vote for a ticket of ten new directors, who would be more liberal in their views than the ministers. Rev. Quigg attempted to counter with attendees and proxies more favorable to his positions. As Bishop Scott, Quigg, Todd, and Will watched helplessly, the Bright/Hooper ticket outnumbered the Quigg ticket by a one hundred and seventy-five to sixty margin, and the slate of business-minded directors was elected. On the question of dancing and other amusements in Rehoboth, the Wilmington newspapers would declare that the "Sinners" had defeated the "Saints."

EARLY THE NEXT morning, Will rode Gideon down to the Bright.

He found George already chomping on a cigar as he supervised the cleanup and rearrangement of the furniture in the parlor from the prior evening's festivities.

"Good mornin', little brother." George sounded gleeful. "I heard about Mr. Bright's victory yesterday. That should resolve what kind of town Rehoboth's goin' to be. You better get on board with that."

"I just came to thank you for tellin' me about my father," Will said as George sat down in an overstuffed chair to rest.

"I could've told you sooner, but I almost never see you. You should come down here in the evenings and have some fun."

Will sat down in a straight back wooden chair across from George. "You know I can't do that. But I would like to have a meal with you sometime and talk about old times on the farm and in the war."

"Maybe when the summer's done and I'm not so busy here," George allowed. "Mr. Bright is rewardin' me for my hard work with tickets to horse racin' in Wilmington next Saturday and a room at one of his hotels. I'll be takin' the train back on Sunday mornin' if you want to go."

"Thanks. I'd like that, but I can't be away on Sunday," said Will. "I'm preachin' at Bethel."

"Well, that's your problem. I know you must be lonely since you're not keepin' company with the pretty organist lady no more. We have some fine lookin' young single ladies from Wilmington stayin' at the Bright who you might want to get to know, if you get what I mean," George said with a wink.

"I'm just fine, and I'm not interested in that kind of woman,"

Will said with conviction. "I do want you to know that I don't hold anythin' against you. I understand now why you never treated me like a full blood brother. I hope you'll find your way back to Bethel church."

"Nope, that ship has sailed. But I do appreciate you comin' by to talk. I've got to go and check on those ladies from Wilmington to make sure they're payin' their rent." George winked again as he turned and climbed the stairs.

IT WAS A hot and hazy late-July Sunday morning in Lewes. Will stood by the front door shaking hands with the worshippers as they departed Bethel Church after the eleven o'clock service. They smiled and thanked him for his thought-provoking sermon. He had preached on the story of Cain and Abel in Genesis Chapter Four, asking the congregation, "Am I My Brother's Keeper?"

As the last worshipper left, Will heard the train's whistle and wondered if George was on it coming back from his trip to Wilmington. He limped the three blocks to the station, arriving just after the southbound train had pulled in. There was a commotion on the platform as a crowd gathered. Four men were carrying a limp body covered with a blanket from the locomotive to a waiting wagon that Will recognized as belonging to Digger Jones, the undertaker.

"What happened?" Will asked the train's engineer, who was standing on the platform shaking.

"One of the passengers tried to move between the cars as we was coming into Georgetown." The engineer's voice trembled. "Somebody said he wanted to get off quick and buy some cigars at the Union Hotel on the Circle. They said he appeared to be drunk, missed his step, and fell between the cars while we was still moving."

"That's terrible," said Will as his heart raced. He felt sick to his stomach. "Do you know his name?"

"I don't. It weren't my fault, but I feel awful cause it happened on my train."

Will limped over to the undertaker's wagon and spoke with O'Dell, who lifted the blanket for him to look. Will fell to his knees when he saw what was left of his brother.

Chapter Thirty-Four

SURPRISE

March 1880

"I'M SO SORRY to hear about your brother," Rev. Todd said as he caught up with Will after the morning session at the annual conference in Dover. "Reverend England told me about it this morning. How are you doing?"

"It's been hard," Will admitted in a low voice with his head bowed. "I had to see his crushed body and then make the arrangements for his funeral and burial on our family farm. Hardly anyone came, not even his wife and son. Only Mr. Bright, Mr. Burton, and some ladies from the hotel. So sad."

"I wish I'd known sooner. What can I do to help you now?"

"Thanks for askin', but I just need to get over it," Will said with resignation. "I'm glad you encouraged me to try and make it right with him last summer. I did meet with him."

"How did that go?"

"He asked me to go with him to watch horse racin' in Wilmington the weekend of his accident," Will said. "I've replayed in my mind a hundred times whether my bein' with him on the train would've made a difference."

"You can't change the past, Will, and it's not your fault," Todd said, stroking his beard. "But you can thank God for what George helped you learn in this life and listen for God's cues moving forward to help others."

"I'm guessin' sometimes it's the hard people and events in our lives that help teach us grace," Will replied, thinking that he was starting to sound like his mentor.

"That's right," said Todd. "And you showed grace and love to your brother even though he may not have deserved it. It's the same way God showers us undeserving souls with grace and love."

"It helps to have that way of lookin' at things. What's happenin' with the camp meetin' this summer?" asked Will.

"It's changing. Last October, the association's new board of directors voted to separate the camp meeting from the association and then lease the grove this summer to the presiding elder of the Dover district for purposes of holding a camp meeting."

"Who's the bishop goin' to appoint as the presidin' elder?" asked Will.

"That would be me," Todd said with a smile.

"Do you need help with the camp meetin'?"

"Of course I hope you can attend," Todd said. "But we're not referring to it as a camp meeting anymore. It'll be called a picnic under religious auspices, with mostly ministers in the conference attending."

"Why's that?"

"As you know, the conference has set some new guidelines for camp meetings that I'm not sure all the attendees are ready to observe. Times are changing, and camp meetings are getting a bad reputation of late."

"I see," said Will, recalling what Bright's lawyer had said at the stockholder's meeting two summers ago. "You probably heard about the Surf House burnin' to the ground last August?"

"Yes, I did," Todd said with regret. "I understand everything except the old parlor piano was destroyed, but thanks be to God that no lives were lost. There were mortgages owing to Mr. Bright, Mr. and Mrs. Martin, and others that hopefully the insurance will pay off and leave some money to invest in a new hotel. But that's no longer a concern of mine or the church. It's not our association any longer."

IN JULY, WILL attended the first service in the brand-new Scott's Chapel that Mr. Hooper and the Rehoboth Beach Association built on Baltimore Avenue. Although it would not be dedicated to Bishop Scott until August, the nondenominational chapel was built in honor to him.

The Chapel was an impressive wooden structure that could seat more than 300. Will wondered why it was not named Todd's Chapel, but was happy to see at least one of the Methodist camp meeting preachers was being honored by the "new" association. He thought maybe this was a peace offering from the businessmen to the ministers, who had been removed from the board by the stockholders.

Scott's Chapel on Baltimore Avenue (undated, courtesy of Delaware Public Archives).

The "religious picnic" had opened five days earlier, and most of the tent houses were empty. There were no advertised services at the grove, only an evening prayer meeting for the thirty families gathered, most of whom were connected to conference ministers.

One Wilmington newspaper was quick to call the Rehoboth camp meeting a "failure" and questioned whether Ocean City seemed to be taking the lead as a summer resort because of Rehoboth's Methodist influence or its inferior train service. Another tabloid challenged Rev. Todd to welcome having a camp meeting next to the sinners so he could convert them.

The newspapers also reported that balls and hops were being held regularly at the Bright House. One Saturday evening, at Rev. Todd's request, Will rode Gideon to the Bright to observe the festivities and report back. He slipped in a back door to avoid being seen.

The orchestra was playing, and ladies wearing long dresses with bustles and men in dark tailored suits with vests were waltzing across the parlor floor. From a distance, Will could hear the accomplished piano player leading the orchestra's dance number. He thought of Susanna and wondered if she was still playing at St. Peter's Church in Lewes.

Will edged his way closer to observe the ten-piece orchestra. He couldn't believe what he saw. The well-dressed man playing the piano appeared to be a younger version of himself. Was he dreaming, or could it be Willie?

Chapter Thirty-Five

SILVER DOLLARS

WILL WAS DUMBSTRUCK. He moved closer and studied the pianist's facial features and mannerisms. It had to be the son he hadn't seen or heard from in seven years. When the orchestra took a break, Will limped over to the piano and stared speechless at his son in his white tie and shirt and black tails.

"Hello, Pop. It's been a long time," Will said calmly. "How are you?"

Will reached out his arms and offered a hug to his son, who turned sideways and extended an arm over his father's shoulder.

"What in the world are you doin' here?" Will asked.

"Adam and I've been playing in the orchestra here all summer, just like we did last year. I thought Uncle George would've told you."

"Your uncle knew you were here?"

"Of course. He knew everyone in the orchestra. I heard he had a bad accident."

Will wondered what else George had failed to tell him but realized what was more important now was that his son had come home, or at least back to Rehoboth for the summer.

"That's right. We buried him up on the farm. Where you stayin'?"

"Mr. Burton gave Adam and me a nice room up on the third floor."

A young man came over with a trumpet.

"Pop, this is my good friend, Adam Johnson. He's an incredible trumpeter."

"I remember you from the camp meetin'. Nice to see you again," Will said, shaking Adam's hand.

"Your son's amazing on the piano. You should stay and hear him play his Chopin sonata after the break," said Adam.

"I might just do that."

When the orchestra leader returned with the other musicians, Will retreated to the back of the room. He watched Willie take a seat at the piano and confidently and flawlessly play what he recognized as a Chopin piece that Elizabeth used to play in their parlor. The audience gave Willie a standing ovation as Will left the parlor and headed back to the campground.

"WHAT'S GOING ON at the Bright?" asked Rev. Todd, who was packing to leave as Will entered the preachers' lodge.

"You won't believe who's playin' the piano in the orchestra," Will exclaimed.

"I wouldn't know who, but it must be someone you do," Todd said with a grin.

"It's my son, Willie, who I've not seen in seven years," said Will. "He's very talented on the piano."

"I remember Willie. He helped save you on the road to Zoar and spent the night with you in my tent house there."

"That's right. He's stayin' with his friend at the Bright and was there all last summer, but George never told me." Will pounded his fist on the table. "I think he and Adam are more than just friends."

"How's that?"

"I don't think they're interested in women. I always thought Willie was different," said Will with frustration.

Rev. Todd hesitated and stroked his beard. "You know God loves all his children, and Jesus teaches us to do the same."

"But I just don't understand how Willie could want to be with another man," Will said. "That's a crime against nature."

"That may be true under our legal system and culture, but God's perspective could be different," Todd said as he removed his glasses. "We're all different in certain ways, and there are some impulses each of us find difficult to resist."

"But how do I treat Willie, especially when Adam is with him?"

"You just have to love him as your son. You may not like everything he does, but he longs to be accepted as your son."

"That's goin' to be hard to do. I expected Willie to be like me."

"Pray about it, and ask God what you should do. And put yourself in Willie's shoes."

THE "PREACHERS' PICNIC" had vacated the campground, and Will came late and sat in the back of Scott's Chapel on Sunday morning. He pondered how to respond to the events of the prior day. He was surprised to see Willie and Adam sitting together up front. Will felt relieved that Willie was alive and well but still concerned about how to make sense of his relationship with Adam in Biblical terms.

Rev. Baer from Washington was at the pulpit preaching about righteousness from the first chapter of Paul's letter to the Romans. He recited from the scripture: "For the wrath of God is revealed from Heaven against all ungodliness and unrighteousness of men . . . including men, leaving the natural use of the woman, burned in their lust one toward another, men with men working that which is unseemly, and receiving in themselves that recompence of their error which was meet." There were shouts of "amen brother" from some of the men in the pews.

A chill went down Will's spine as he watched Willie and Adam shift uncomfortably in their seats. There must be more, Will thought as he flipped through his Bible to Galatians 3:28 and read: "There is neither Jew nor Greek, there is neither bond nor free, there is neither male nor female: for ye are all one in Christ Jesus." Will wondered how this verse could be reconciled with the Romans passage when written by the same man of God. Wasn't Paul telling us that in Christ we are all the same and equal to one another?

After the service, Will walked down Baltimore Avenue to the boardwalk. He marveled at the immensity of the ocean before him as the midday sun sparkled on its calm surface beyond the breaking waves. Will likened this beautiful and broad creation to the unconditional love he had experienced from others, including Elizabeth and Rev. Todd. He sat on the dune and closed his eyes in prayer.

After twenty minutes of meditation, he knew what he had to do.

Will limped down the boardwalk to the Bright House, where he found Willie sitting alone on the front porch watching the surf break. Adam was swimming in the deep water.

"Son, I was very impressed with your solo last night."

"Oh, did you stay to listen?" asked Willie.

"I sure did, and I saw the applause you received."

Willie blushed. "I guess all those piano lessons Mama gave me have paid off. I'm sorry I couldn't make her funeral."

"Did you get my telegram?"

"I did, but it came late. I don't know if I could've seen her lowered into the ground," Willie said as he began to tear up.

"She was a fine mother and wife," said Will, reaching for his handkerchief to give to Willie.

"Yes, she was. I really miss her. Did she suffer?"

"Not too much. We got her some medicine for the pain, and the Lord took her quickly." Will paused to collect himself. "Why'd you leave home and not let us know where to find you?"

"I knew I wasn't the son you wanted me to be, so I had to find out who I really am." Willie blew his nose with the handkerchief.

"Did you?"

"I think so. I'm very happy with Adam." Willie reached into his pocket and pulled out five silver dollars. "Here's the money I borrowed when I left home."

"You don't need to pay me back," said Will. "I'm just glad to see you again and know you're okay. Do you plan to stay in Rehoboth?"

"No. We'll be heading back to Philadelphia in September, and we're going to New York City next month with a small group of musicians to play chamber music at Steinway Hall. That's where the best orchestras in New York usually perform."

"Good Lord. You're becomin' really famous. I'm proud of you, Willie. I'm sorry I treated you so bad growin' up."

Willie looked away as he fought his tears. "I'd like it if you'd come watch Adam and me perform there," he said, looking up at his father.

"You tell me when, and I'll be there. You, Adam, and I will have a fine dinner at one of those fancy New York restaurants, now that we have five silver dollars to spend." Will grinned and embraced his son. Willie smiled as his father slowly descended the porch stairs to leave.

Chapter Thirty-Six

DISAPPOINTMENT

July 1881

"THIS LOOKS LIKE the end of our church's control in Rehoboth," said Rev. Todd grimacing as he stroked his beard.

He and Will were seated in the tabernacle, where the stockholders of the Rehoboth Beach Association had just voted to adopt changes to the charter approved by the Delaware Legislature five months earlier. The charter had been revised to delete the prohibition of everything inconsistent with Christian morality as taught by the Methodist Episcopal Church.

Rehoboth Beach was no longer constrained by the church.

"We could still have a gatherin' in the grove for the preachers and those church families who agree to abide by the conference's rules," Will said hopefully.

"Rehoboth is no longer the Christian seaside resort I had

envisioned," said Todd with a hint of resignation in his voice. "The train stops right at our front gate bringing people who have no interest in attending a revival. They'd rather go to the Bright where they can dance or engage in other secular amusements. They want to bring their malts and liquor and have a gay old time at the seashore."

"But what if we keep holdin' camp meetings and draw some of those who came for worldly pursuits to our services so they can hear the message and be saved?" Will asked.

"I'm deeply concerned it will work the opposite way," Todd responded. "If we continue, we're likely to lose some faithful Christians when they're exposed to the heathen practices now going on here. Have you seen those ladies in their provocative bathing costumes lying on the beach? I even heard there are prostitutes plying their trade at the Bright. The businessmen have allowed the devil to get a foothold and spoil what we worked so hard to establish here."

Rev. Todd's disappointment was palpable, and Will felt like he had let his mentor down. He didn't know what to say that would console Todd.

"Let's think and pray about this some more," Will offered.

"As the presiding elder of our Dover district, I need to talk to the bishop," Todd said firmly. "The conference has invested a lot of time and resources in this camp meeting venture, so it's not up to you and me to determine what happens next."

DISAPPOINTMENT

WILL LEFT THE campground feeling dejected. He rode Gideon to the post office in Robinson's Boarding House on Rehoboth Avenue. There was a letter there for him from Willie, postmarked New York City. Willie and Adam hadn't returned to Rehoboth for the summer. Their performance at Steinway Hall back in the fall had led to other engagements there and in other New York venues.

Will opened the letter and read that Willie and Adam had rented a flat on Fourteenth Street just off Union Square and were enjoying the cultural scene in Manhattan. The letter recounted the many concerts he and Adam had played, and those scheduled in the months ahead. He read with satisfaction that they were worshipping at the John Street Methodist-Episcopal Church in Lower Manhattan.

Will missed seeing his son but was pleased that he seemed happy with his career and his relationship with Adam, and that the faith he and Elizabeth had instilled in Willie was still alive. He realized he'd underestimated Willie's potential and was glad he'd made peace with his son last summer.

THE NEXT WEEK, Will rode Gideon to Lewes and met with Rev. Prettyman, the pastor recently assigned to Bethel Church where Will continued to serve as a local preacher.

"Reverend Todd thinks the camp meetin's have run their course in Rehoboth," Will related to Prettyman as he laid his Bible on the desk in the tiny office where he'd received instruction from Rev. Pegg six years earlier. "Todd says it's up to the bishop to decide what happens next, but I feel like it's my fault for not stoppin' what goes on at the hotels and boardin' houses."

"I'm sure it's a disappointment to Todd," Prettyman observed, "but you did what you could to help the camp meeting flourish. Maybe it's time for a new season to blossom in your life."

"What do you mean?" asked Will.

Prettyman leaned back in his desk chair and took off his glasses. "Reverend England told me about how you rallied the Nanticokes to attend the camp meeting two years ago. They need a new pastor at Israel Church as Reverend Hill is retiring. Are you up for it?"

"But what about my duties here at Bethel?" asked Will.

"We have a new young local preacher from Lewes who the conference has assigned to Bethel," Prettyman said directly.

"You're sayin' I've been replaced?" Will asked incredulously.

Prettyman cleared his throat. "Look at this as a temporary

assignment at Israel to see if you like it. I've checked with the presiding elder in our district, and he agrees it's a good opportunity for you."

"Presidin' elder? You mean Reverend Todd?"

"Yes. He told me your work at the Rehoboth camp meeting was likely coming to an end."

Will grabbed his Bible, tucked it under his left arm, and charged out of Prettyman's office without saying another word. He felt abandoned by his mentor and his church. As he came around the corner to untie and mount Gideon for the trip home, he was met by a woman he hadn't seen for five years.

Susanna was wearing an attractive flowery summer dress and red lipstick. "Hello, Will. It's been a long time. I'm glad I ran into you."

The memories of Elizabeth's death and Mathew's accident came flooding back. Will didn't know what to say. He threw up his arms in frustration and his Bible fell to the ground. "God, why is this happenin' to me?" he yelled looking up to the heavens.

Will untied Gideon and jerked the reins so hard that the horse backed up in fear. As he mounted and rode off, he saw Susanna pick up his Bible lying in the street and shrugged his shoulders.

Chapter Thirty-Seven

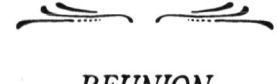

REUNION

August 1881

WILL LIMPED EASTWARD along Brooklyn Avenue toward the ocean. The first hint of sunrise emerged on the horizon, and the thin wispy clouds were beginning to receive color as if from a hidden artist. Clutching a paper in his hand, Will crossed Surf Avenue and stood for a minute on the narrow boardwalk squinting to see the pastels develop before him.

He was drawn to the beach and surf just as he had been many times before when he needed solace and healing from the wounds of shame, injury, and difficult people in his midst. So much had happened in the last ten years. Will's mind drifted to past regrets, and his mood turned melancholy.

As the sand gave way under his weak knee and Will struggled to cross the modest dune before him, he saw the dark sky across the Atlantic giving way to light. The airborne gulls nearby interrupted the melodic rhythm of the waves with their screeching cries signaling the morning catch to their comrades. Going slowly, he managed to scale the sand mound and sat down with a thud on its downward slope to rest and meditate before the unpleasant events of the day unfolded.

A light breeze from the southwest told him the morning was going to be hot and humid with maybe a squall in the afternoon or early evening. But right now, as the sun peeked up from the horizon, the temperature felt comfortable, almost cool, and Will pulled his coat closer and faced northeast to keep the breeze at his back. The pink sunrise brought back memories of a similar morning eight years earlier, when he couldn't sleep because of the excitement of the first camp meeting in Rehoboth.

It was much different now, as he thought back to what had happened since he first came to this place named after a Biblical plain in Israel. "How can a merciful God ordain all that has happened here?" mused Will as he recalled the events leading up to the telegram he held in his hand.

Will had received it the day before. Short and to the point, it read: "Rev. Thompson STOP The Conference leadership has voted to suspend the summer encampment at Rehoboth Beach for an indefinite period STOP Please make all necessary arrangements to secure and return all Conference materials immediately STOP Yours in Christ Bishop Simpson STOP"

In some respects, the bishop's telegram was understandable. What had begun by his mentor Rev. Todd as a large and exciting assemblage of worshippers gathered for spiritual revival had drifted into a small gathering of preachers as the train came to town and the businessmen took over the association. Now Rehoboth was known for its dancing, drinking, card-playing, and available women at the Bright House.

Still, the abruptness of the bishop's telegram sent shivers down Will's spine. Had someone disclosed to him the unfounded rumors of Will's liaison with Susanna? Had the stories about Matthew's hunting accident or his brother's work at the Bright reached the leaders of the Methodist-Episcopal Conference? Did the conference know his son was another man's lover? If so, the termination of the summer camp meeting in Rehoboth might be the least of his worries. He could lose his local preacher's license and be shamed in front of Rev. Todd and the rest of the conference.

For a fleeting instant, he pondered walking into the surf over his head and ending this misery. It would be so easy and fast, since he couldn't swim a stroke. Would he even be missed?

He looked out at the water. He could make out the silhouette of a lone fisherman standing in the surf about 100 yards to the north. He didn't know who it was as his eyes were failing and he was having great difficulty lately recognizing folks until they were very close.

As the sun now seemed to race out of the water, it was turning yellow, and a gleaming ribbon of light was forming on the sea before him. Was it a sign beckoning him home, he wondered almost aloud.

Just then a voice broke his trance. It was the sweet high-pitched tone of a woman asking, "Will?" She sounded at once angelic and yet familiar. He turned his gaze from the sunrise unfolding before him and realized it was Susanna. His first thought was why had she come back after all that had happened. But he soon realized that she had been sent by another.

"Are you all right?" she asked.

"What are you doin' here?"

"I was worried about you after I saw you in Lewes last week. I brought this back." She offered him his Bible.

"I won't be needin' it anymore," Will said, looking with disdain at the worn black-covered book he had spent so much time with in recent years.

"That's not what Reverend Prettyman told me."

"Why are you talkin' to him?"

"I went to visit him after I saw you last week. He told me how to find Reverend Todd's cottage here, and I also spoke to him."

"About me?"

"Yes."

"It's none of your business."

"Yes it is, Will, because I care about you. It's never as bad as you might think."

"Well, it's pretty awful for me right now. And you said you never wanted to see me again after what happened to Matthew."

"I was very upset," said Susanna, making eye contact with Will. "Later, I learned from Matthew that it wasn't your fault and that you saved his life when he almost drowned out here."

"How's he doin'?" Will asked.

"He's much better," she said with a smile. "He's able to use his arm again. And he's studying to become a preacher. He asks about you often."

"What did Todd tell you?" asked Will.

"He said the bishop was going to end the camp meetings in Rehoboth but you were being offered a new opportunity to lead another church nearby. He was very excited for you. Reverend Todd thinks highly of you and wants you to stay in the ministry. He said you are the perfect pastor for your new church. And he plans to ask you to do some preaching at Scott's Chapel next summer."

Will paused and tried to take in all he had just heard. He shook his head and looked out to the watery expanse in front of him and then glanced upwards to the heavens. Maybe he was the right man to pastor Israel Church given his background. He turned his gaze to Susanna and reached up to grasp her outstretched hand.

"You were sent as God's messenger to help save me from myself," he said as a tear ran down his cheek. "The Lord knew I needed to hear what you just said. I guess there's room enough for me to continue preachin' in Rehoboth."

"I know that God isn't finished with us yet," Susanna said as she sat down next to Will. She handed him his Bible and kissed him on the cheek.

"I was so upset when I saw you in Lewes last week. I guess I'll still be needin' the Good Book after all," Will said, grasping his Bible firmly.

The sun was now fully above the horizon, the wind had shifted, and there was a pleasant breeze coming off the ocean. Together they watched the surf fisherman reel in three striped bass as they talked about what had happened to each of them since they had been close five years earlier. Seagulls flew overhead, laughing as they scanned the beach for fragments of food.

AUTHOR'S POSTSCRIPT

I developed an interest in what life was like in Rehoboth 150 years ago in 2014 when I began appearing in costume as Rev. Robert Todd for the Rehoboth Beach Historical Society and met "campers" at the Anna Hazzard Tent House Museum on Christian Street in Rehoboth Beach. It is an original camp meeting tent house from the 1890s and is located a stone's throw from Lorenzo Dow Martin's farmhouse. Research for *Room Enough* began as I sought to learn more about Rev. Todd and the founding of my hometown. As with any historical novel, this book attempts to weave a story with fictional characters into the known events of the era. In researching *Room Enough*, I was fortunate to have newspapers and books to rely upon for factual information and discover details about actual persons who appear in the book, including Rev. Todd, Rev. Quigg, Rev. Warner, Rev. Pegg, Rev. England, Rev. Prettyman, Rev. Stevenson, Bishop Scott, Lorenzo Dow Martin, Catherine "Kitty" Martin, John Marsh, William Bright, and William Hooper.

While Will Thompson and his family are fictional, the 1868 Delaware State Atlas of Lewes and Rehoboth depicts a farmhouse owned by W.P. Thompson adjacent to a farmhouse owned by

Lorenzo Dow Martin. The Martin farmhouse still exists on what is now the southeast corner of Christian Street and Scarborough Avenue in Rehoboth Beach. It is believed that the Thompson farm, which bordered on Newbolds Freshwater Lake (now Silver Lake), became the Rehoboth Beach Country Club in 1925 with a nine-hole golf course and is now known as Country Club Estates.

Doc Marsh is fictional, while Dr. Hall was a real doctor in Lewes in the 1870s. Susanna and Matthew Robinson, Adam Johnson, Elijah Miller and his family, John Hudson and Isaac Hill and his family are fictional. The Bethel, Israel, St. George, and Midway Presbyterian churches and Scott's Chapel are real, as is the Zoar church and its former camp meeting site.

The grounds of the Rehoboth Beach Camp Meeting are depicted as shown in the July 1873 *Rehoboth Beacon* published by the Rehoboth Beach Camp Meeting Association and other publications of that era. The streets, camp grounds, tabernacle, Surf House, Bright House, and Railroad Depot are real, although it is not clear when the tabernacle was constructed. The Cape Henlopen Lighthouse, Beacon Light, United States Hotel, steamer pier, and train station in Lewes all existed during the period.

Although certain characters are real and care has been taken to present them as described in historical documents, scenes involving them are fictional or have been embellished. For example, it is not known if Rev. Todd attended the Zoar Camp Meeting in 1872, had a handicapped daughter or a horse named Gideon, although all of these are possible. Likewise, we don't know if Lorenzo Dow Martin's first encounter with Rev. Todd involved a shotgun or whether Kitty Martin played her organ at the first camp meeting. William Bright had a significant influence on the founding and development of Rehoboth Beach, but it is not known whether he kept a flask in his suit coat or had a piano player as part of the orchestra performing at the Bright House.

In other cases, events reported in newspapers of the time have been superimposed on our characters. A man was struck by lightning and killed during the building of a cottage next to the Surf House in 1873. Another man lost his life on the train coming to Lewes when he fell between two cars. Tuberculosis and malaria were prevalent diseases during the 1870s. These events help tell the story of the founding of Rehoboth, even if they didn't all happen. I hope you enjoyed reading about them as much as I did envisioning them.

W.R.T.

Key Reference Materials

Rehoboth Beacon (Rehoboth Beach, DE), 1873, 1876, 1877 available at the Rehoboth Beach Historical Museum

Morning News (Wilmington, DE), *News Journal* (Wilmington, DE), *Daily Republican* (Wilmington, DE), *Delaware State Journal* (Wilmington, DE), *Daily Gazette* (Wilmington, DE), *Delaware Tribune* (Wilmington, DE), *Wilmington Daily Commercial* (Wilmington, DE), *Morning Herald* (Wilmington, DE), *Smyrna Times* (Smyrna, DE), *Evening Star* (Washington, D.C.), *Baltimore Sun* (Baltimore, MD), *Philadelphia Inquirer* (Philadelphia, PA), *Philadelphia Times* (Philadelphia, PA), *Democratic Advocate* (Westminster, MD), *Star-Democrat* (Easton, MD), *Cecil Whig* (Elkton, MD), 1871-81. Available via www.newspapers.com

Minutes of the Wilmington Conference of the Methodist Episcopal Church, 1872-81, available at www.barrattschapel.org

Methodism of the Peninsula, Rev. Robert W. Todd, 1886

The Garden of American Methodism: The Delmarva Peninsula 1769-1820, William H. Williams, 1984

*Cultivating the Methodist Garden, a brief history of the Peninsu-

la-Delaware Conference of the United Methodist Church, Barbara Duffin and Philip Lawton, 2000

Wide Views and a Loving Heart, The Life and Ministry of Bishop Levi Scott, Joseph F. DiPaolo, 2018

Delaware's Forgotten Folk, The Story of the Moors & Nanticokes, C.S. Weslager, 1943

My Business was to Fight the Devil, Recollections of Rev. Adam Wallace, Peninsula Circuit Rider, Joseph F. DiPaolo, 1998

Methodism in Rehoboth Beach, John Gauger, 2018

Lorenzo Dow Martin, Seaside Farm, and Rehoboth's Founding, Paul D. Lovett, Journal of the Lewes Historical Society, Vol XXIV, 2021

History of Delaware, 1609-1888, J. Thomas Scharf, 1888

Made in the USA
Middletown, DE
26 June 2023

33761336R10170